VAMPIRE WARS

THE
VALKYRIES

Heather
Knox

EPIC Escape

An Imprint of EPIC Press
abdopublishing.com

The Valkyries
Vampire Wars: Book #6

abdopublishing.com

Published by EPIC Press, a division of ABDO, PO Box 398166, Minneapolis, Minnesota 55439. Copyright © 2019 by Abdo Consulting Group, Inc. International copyrights reserved in all countries. No part of this book may be reproduced in any form without written permission from the publisher. Escape™ is a trademark and logo of EPIC Press.

Printed in the United States of America, North Mankato, Minnesota.

062018
092018

Cover design by Candice Keimig
Images for cover and interior art obtained from iStockphoto.com
Edited by Jennifer Skogen

Library of Congress Cataloging-in-Publication Data

Library of Congress Control Number: 2018932900

Publisher's Cataloging in Publication Data

Names: Knox, Heather, author.
Title: The valkyries/ by Heather Knox
Description: Minneapolis, MN : EPIC Press, 2019 | Series: Vampire wars; #6
Summary: In the aftermath of the Keeper and Praedari war, Delilah learns from the Council the fate of those Praedari captured: the Ritae Cruciatus, a barbaric set of customs predating the Praedari. Delilah must make a choice between two people she once loved: Will she save Victor from his Final Moment, or honor the memory and unlife's work of Zeke? Of course, the Valkyries may have other plans for her—and Delilah's not the only one with a past.
Identifiers: ISBN 9781680769098 (lib. bdg.) | ISBN 9781680769371 (ebook)
Subjects: LCSH: Vampires--Fiction. | War--Fiction--Fiction. | Prisoners of war--Fiction--Fiction. | Moral responsibility--Fiction | Young adult fiction.
Classification: DDC [FIC]--dc23

For Sylvia Quinn

Now

Six Elders where seven once sat around a gleaming mahogany table without blemish. Leland stands at the head of the table opposite where Enoch the Gray sits, four of the remaining seats occupied, his own, nearest the door, empty: Alistair, Evelyn, Brantley and, the reason they've gathered, Temperance.

It's not that none of the assembled Elders notice the strangeness of her dress this evening, but that none dare mention it. She wears something like Victorian mourning clothes: all black, her blouse a bloom of lace at her throat, layers of swishing black skirts bustled at the back. Even her hands are covered with black lace gloves, her face hidden behind a veil. Her long chestnut hair pinned in an elegant updo, tucked underneath part of the veil, to which the veil attaches with a black diamond-encrusted comb, the only thing that could be said to be of this era.

Around her throat, on top of the fabric of the dress and falling at her fossa jugularis sternalis, the jugular notch where the clavicle meets, a small vial filled with red: a Victorian lachrymosa, the tear-catcher thought to mark the end of the mourning period when the mourner's tears within evaporated.

"Your informant has delivered the message?" Leland asks, addressing Temperance.

"Yes." The word is but a slip of air rustling the black veil that hides her features, but somehow they all still hear it, the weight of it hanging in the air between them.

"And the girl has made contact?"

"She has." Temperance allows herself a dip of the head, emphasizing her response.

"Why did we have to wait?" Brantley interrupts, reclining in his seat with his hands behind his head and feet propped up on the table, crossed at the ankle.

"We needed the Crusader to bring Delilah to Ismae," Alistair explains, annoyed.

And with more patience than Brantley deserves, Temperance thinks. She wants to slap Brantley— Brantley who never seems to listen unless someone is offering him praise. They've been over this. They've debated this. So many Everlasting say an hour, a day, a month, even a year feels like nothing, but they've never debated the minutiae of magic and politics and warfare with this Council.

She wants to offer his service to Evelyn as she continues to lose herself to the ritual that shall awaken Ismae the Bloody, so that Brantley may face the same gruesome end as her beloved assistant, Nikolai. Poor Nikolai, carved up like a pumpkin,

Evelyn cowering in the corner, muttering and waving a bloody knife at Temperance, who found her. *Heart and lung, heart and lung, heart and lung, heart and lung.* Poor thing, though Nikolai intended to carve her up so she beat him to the punch. Poor thing will never be the same.

But that is not why the Council voted to wait. Her own informant could not risk their cover, insisting to be brought to Ismae, so they maneuvered Delilah into place to confirm her location. As soon as Delilah made contact, her informant brought Victor the information about the mistranslation. Temperance knew there was no way Delilah would let her Usher's Usher from her sight. Even if Delilah believed the stories, that Ismae the Bloody was the first Praedari, she's too much like Ezekiel to miss her Awakening. Which was a favor the Council surely owed Delilah for her service.

"Doesn't your informant know where they keep Ismae? Isn't that the point of an informant?" But

Brantley doesn't press it, a sharp look from Alistair silencing him.

She wants to tell Brantley that her informant isn't planning on returning alive, such is their service. She wants to reach across the table and grab him by the throat and scream in his face until the weight of what it means to serve the Council pulls him so far into himself that his predator within rends his flesh into strips with fang and claw, devours his organs. She wants to, but instead she regards him coolly from underneath her veil.

Later, she tells herself. *You shall handle him later. You shall make him understand—make him* feel *every loss, every drop of blood and Blood lost.* And Delilah? And Lydia? How to make someone as self-involved as Brantley understand that each body they tally among the dead—or lost—was a person?

Enough. It all unfolds as it must. A voice without body, but they all know it to be Enoch the Gray. He tilts his head in a single nod to Leland.

"Congratulations, Council," Leland says with

too-easy a smile; but it's his way and she does not fault him that. "We are at war."

2

Now

*H*E KNOWS I NEED YOUR HEART AND LUNG, *Childe, don't you see? He's sent you here to die.*

But before I can answer there's a rumbling off in the distance, beyond the cellar we're in. Like an earthquake, I can feel the sway of the building, of the stone floor and four stone walls rocking. Not quite the sense of being tossed about at sea but of watching the sea rage against the vessel containing you, that dizziness of falling were you not contained. Like an earthquake, this sense of the entire earth splitting open, the one thing we should be able to rely on turning against us, tearing in two, a broken home. Outside this cellar, outside this storm I've become: the siege has begun. I feel it in my bones before I hear it because her words fill my rational thought.

Then: *What's left is earthquake,* I think. *Earthquake. But surely Victor never meant me to die?*

ে৻৶

Fifteen minutes earlier: "Things with the others are escalating. I don't think it's safe for you here anymore," Victor says, looking into my eyes, worry clouding his already-gray ones. "I can't be everywhere at once, and it's difficult to know who to trust." He steps in closer, his look inviting defiance, hoping for some push back, or bracing for it. "You should go, before something happens. You can take one of the trucks. No one will follow you."

I do not hesitate, do not pause: "No."

"I-I'm sorry?" The wide-eyed stun of someone not used to hearing no.

"I said no. I want to stay. I'm not done here."

"Delilah . . ."

"You told me I've always been stubborn, why would that be any different now?"

He shakes his head, stepping in closer and reaching for my hands. I cannot feel the warmth of his body so close to mine because we wear the tepid flesh of the undead, but there's the distinct buzz of *something*, of what once was, or what could be. Maybe the mingling of our auras, where they overlap, a phenomenon some Everlasting claim they can sense or see. The sensation starts at my core and radiates outwards, up and down my spine in unison, circling my waist where I wish his hands would wander, and I shudder just slightly. I can almost feel the cool brush of goosebumps breaking out over my skin, though they do not, while the predator within me smirks, lying satisfied in wait. Her impulse to kill sated by a promise, she'll allow me this. So long spent straddling the two worlds of the Keepers and the Praedari has taught me how to bargain with her—my beast.

Victor opens his mouth to speak but I cut him off.

"Come inside?" I look up at him from lowered lashes, lean in.

"Victor!" The smooth timbre of Pierce's voice rolls in and instantly he's come upon us, clapping Victor on the back in greeting. "Victor, just who I was looking for. Do you have a minute?"

He lets go of my hands, an apology to me marring the smile he flashes Pierce, but Pierce does not seem to notice—already leading Victor down the hall and chattering away about something. It seems like no matter where we are, Pierce is there too.

"How long has he known?" I ask. "You!" I step towards Lydia, fists balled at my side, but the movement is cut short as I clutch my head, still reeling from coming into contact with my Usher's Usher, the ancient source of my Heartsblood. "You knew he needed my heart and lung? How long?" The questions drip from my lips as half-whimpers.

It doesn't make sense: why would Victor insist I leave and then bring me down to this cellar to die? Was it a test? Did he find out during that short time between us speaking and—Pierce. Pierce spoke to him and then Victor sent me and Lydia down here. I snarl again at her, closing in on her and forcing her back to the wall.

She takes a step backwards into the wall, hands in front of her as if in surrender. "Are you okay? What just happened? I swear I had no idea." Lydia crosses her arms over her chest. "Well, okay. I had no idea who *you* were, I've only just put that together—you must be related to Ismae the Bloody? That's *incredible*! She's the first Praedari, Delilah! That means *you* have her Blood! That—" She gestures to the doorway I collapsed in. "That must've been because of your connection to her? I've heard about that—" But a glare in her direction shuts up the tangent she's about to embark upon. "I've known about the issue with the translation for, like, a few hours. Not about you though. I swear. I probably wouldn't have been such a jerk to you if I'd known."

"Am I the only one that hears that?!" Hunter stands near the open door, eyeing the stairs outside it. "Those are explosions. Like the subway tunnel you guys blew up when you *kidnapped* me. For no reason, might I add . . . "

Lydia sighs. "So? Why aren't you running? The door's *open*. You never wanted to be here."

"Because there's vampires out there," he says with a discouraged pout, running a hand on the smooth cement of Ismae's burial vault. "And there's more to the story than you know. We can't leave her."

Lydia scoffs. "Please!" Then she turns to me. "What's the scrawny one talking about? When can I talk to her? I want to meet her!"

He means that I wish *to wake. That I* must *wake. Just as The Crusader intended me to.*

Lydia's eyes grow wide and her hands drop to her sides. "Holy—what?! How did you do that?" She glares at me as though demanding an answer, but none comes. I shrug, savor the moment of gloating, and cross my arms across my chest as hers just were, blocking her access to my Usher's Usher.

"No way. Just—no. No way. Ismae the Bloody talked *to me*! Pierce is never gonna believe this!" She puts her palm to her forehead. She bends at the knees twice in rapid succession, a sort of hop-stomp as the reality of their situation settles over her. "She *wants* to wake up, guys. Delilah, your Elder, your Usher's Usher *needs* to wake up. She's meant to be here, she just told me."

"I heard," I agree, my voice wavering. I find myself amused by her enthusiasm, like a child meeting their favorite baseball player or cartoon character but she has no idea what brought me to my knees when we arrived at the cellar: the stars, the slurry of blood and ash, the limbs, the raven, the web connecting us all.

Confusion, no time to sort through what might be logical or practical, or what is past and what is vision, and whose. For the first time since my Becoming I wish I could pull Lydia into my mind and show someone what Ismae has shown me. I want to hear what someone else thinks—never did I feel this impulse with Zeke because it was something sacred between me and his Usher, something secret that skipped him and found me but somehow it feels as though Lydia should be let in, that she's a part of it.

"I don't mean to interrupt the fun," Hunter starts, glancing between Ismae and the open door of his prison. "They were a ways off but if those explosions mean what Ismae—"

I shake my head. If Ismae has found a need to communicate with the girl, let her. My loyalty is unwavering. "The Keepers have come," I state plainly for the benefit of everyone assembled. "The war has begun. And you . . . " I lock eyes with Lydia. "You are on the wrong side."

Now

CHARLIE WAKES FIRST, CLICKING ON THE TV IN their motel room, sound muted. Next to her Logan snores softly, a sound she grew used to while they roomed at Project Harvest together. On the bed next to theirs, Morgeaux has kicked off all the blankets and sprawls diagonally across the entire expanse of bed, one pillow halfway on the nightstand, face down on the other. She knocked a half-full glass of water onto the carpet but it's hardly the worst this room has seen.

The bed linens smell of bleach, and the bathroom of strong disinfectant—probably what triggered Charlie's restless sleep the night before. She doubts Logan slept well at all until now. They discussed taking watch shifts, three hours long each so that each of them got six hours of sleep, but they decided instead to only take a short break here at this quiet two-star no-tell motel, which was far enough off the interstate that only one other room was occupied. Its occupant likely belonged to the semi parked near the rear of the small parking lot.

Sleep while the vampires sleep, they figured, but they found themselves exhausted from the fight the night before and, according to the clock, the vampires probably beat them awake this time.

She rises and goes to the desk, fills the glass carafe of the cheap coffee maker in the bathroom, tip-toeing so as to let the others sleep. She tears open a pouch of sealed-yet-somehow-stale coffee grounds and empties them into a white paper filter. She clicks the one button on the machine and within a minute the gurgling fills the room, followed by the smell of coffee which she figures will probably wake the others anyway, but at least they'll wake to coffee.

Morgeaux stirs next, sitting up and stretching. She still wears her distressed black skinny jeans and combat boots, her blue-black hair piled on top of her head in a messy bun. None of them had pajamas with them, or even a change of clothes, but Morgeaux had a few things in a smaller bag inside her purse she offered to share: a stick of Old Spice Amber men's deodorant; a pack of spearmint Trident gum; lip balm; some liquid lipsticks, mostly in the same shade of dark purple or purple-black, but different brands and finishes and different stages of emptying; a small rollerball of some perfume like the sample you'd get at Sephora for one hundred Beauty Insider points, a masculine, woodsy-smoky scent; two deluxe-size black mascaras; Kat Von D Tattoo Liner, black; black hair binders. Charlie had rifled through it before retiring to bed for the daylight hours.

Also the day before, as they settled in for bed,

Morgeaux offered Charlie something from the smaller bag to help her sleep, a tiny white pill from an orange bottle bearing her name on the label. She said they were for her own anxiety and PTSD. Ever since they had tried to kidnap her, this often kept her up, but Charlie politely declined, though appreciative of the offer. She wanted to be able to wake for an intruder or something outside should she need to, the heightened awareness of their Blood still in her veins, a boon at times like these—though in retrospect she wished she'd just taken whatever Morgeaux offered so she wouldn't feel so tired right now, her own jumble of memory and nightmares keeping her from sleeping well.

In a way, Charlie wondered if it wasn't worse that Morgeaux had gotten away—facing the constant fear of whether they would come for her again, and with more force. She knows the girl ended up at some safehouse, the details of which grow more sparse each time Morgeaux speaks of it, as if fading from her memory. Still, she couldn't return home, despite not being imprisoned by the Praedari as Charlie, Logan, Kiley, and Hunter had been. And the four of them hadn't been mistreated once they were settled into their suite.

A part of Charlie believed their limited privileges were for their safety. The other Praedari onsite might have harmed them despite being under orders not to. She turns a coffee mug over in her hands, lost in thought.

"Hey!" Morgeaux whispers, pointing next to Charlie at the TV. "Isn't that where you guys were?"

Charlie turns, the too-small white ceramic mug slipping from her hand and hitting the carpet with a muffled thud before rolling another six inches or so.

"Oh my god!" Charlie gasps, steadying herself with a hand on the back of the wooden chair tucked under the desk-table where her coffee pot sputters and chokes.

Logan bolts up at her exclamation, grabbing at the nightstand for the lamp in his startled state, lifting it as if it's a football and he's ready to pitch it. He blinks a few times, Morgeaux staring at him with raised eyebrows and a smirk.

"Huh? What—?" He shakes his head and rubs his eyes with a yawn, setting the lamp back on the nightstand now that the immediate danger has passed.

"What *exactly* were you gonna do with that, big guy?" Morgeaux laughs, crossing her outstretched legs in front of her. "Hey, Charlie, grab me a cuppa, would you?"

"Shhhh!" Charlie scolds, turning the volume on the TV up so she can hear.

Project Harvest is on the screen, unmistakable. The gravel driveway, the row of waiting vehicles. The toolshed where Charlie stole materials for staking when her and Logan went into the yard for the first time to work. The silo. They never figured out what was being stored in the silo, but there it stood, a dark silhouette like other dark silhouettes on the property, illuminated from behind with the occasional flash of light. A haze-like smoke fills the air.

Charlie notices a hole where the garage once connected to the farmhouse.

"We have to go back for them!" Charlie exclaims, gesturing at the TV where a helicopter hovers above the chaos, blowing the reporter's hair into her face.

"Reporting from Ground Zero, it seems the raid on the confirmed cult, Project Harvest, has escalated in force. Leaders refuse to engage with authorities attempting to negotiate for the turning-over of the property and the safe evacuation of those inside into police custody. There's no telling how many members they quietly amassed since they took over this bucolic farmhouse nestled in the—hold on!"

The reporter presses her hand to an earpiece she wears, listening to something and nodding. "It seems they are fighting back, gunfire confirmed, which you can hear behind me—"

"*Now* you want to go back! It's a *raid*, Charlie! There are tanks and explosions and gunfire and—" Logan points at the television where people in hazmat suits wheel a couple stretchers, each with a sheet drawn up over the face of the dead. "Do you have a death wish?" he challenges, tone harsh. "Those are *bodies*. Bodies, not piles of ash. We can't just interfere with a military op—"

"He's right," Morgeaux interjects, stepping towards the two. "But you're not wrong, Charlie. We *do* need to go back for them."

"See? Wait—" Logan spins to face her. "What? What do you mean we *need* to go back for them? How is she not wrong?"

Charlie turns from the TV, too, her eyes wide with surprise as both of them face down Morgeaux, waiting for an explanation.

"They have no way of knowing that Kiley and Hunter aren't a part of the so-called cult. They're hauling bodies out of there—you think they're asking before they shoot? And it's mostly vampires inside, right? So you know they're not using tear gas and rubber bullets—"

"Does the government know they're dealing with vampires, though? Maybe they *are* using crowd control measures," Logan offers. "Do they usually blast into cult bunkers with lethal force?"

"At this point the government either knows and is making a show of force, or whoever initiated the raid knows. Quinn said the Everlasting, especially the Keepers, pull a lot of strings in our world to hide their existence. This could be that. Even if our government refuses to go public with the reality of vampires, plenty of the regular population is ready to believe and ready to take up stakes. The Keepers have some cleaning up to do to protect themselves and the Praedari just don't care."

"Okay, but we can't just run in there and—"

"Absolutely not," Morgeaux cuts him off. "But we can find someone in charge and tell them there are human prisoners."

"More than just Kiley and Hunter," Charlie begins, her voice small. She shakes her head slightly, as if trying to call up something long buried. "Bits of memory from when they treated me started coming back."

"Charlie, you never told us—" Logan leans in, putting a hand on her shoulder but she shrugs it off.

"I didn't want to bother anyone. Besides, I wasn't sure if they were real or hallucinations. It's all hazy and confused—but that doesn't matter now. Even if just some of it is true there are a *lot* of innocent people in there."

"Okay, can we just call 911 and let them handle it? And isn't there like a tip line or something for suspicious activity? I heard it on the radio when they announced the curfew."

Morgeaux shakes her head. "911 has been replaced by a recording. They log your location based on cell towers, but there's almost no chance someone will be dispatched and there's no one manning the line to speak with. It got bad out here and now with the curfew in effect—" She lets the statement hang between them, offering a shrug.

"We have to go," Charlie states.

"We have to go," Logan echoes with a sigh.

"Let's go," Morgeaux says, grabbing the keys.

4

Now

"**R**UN," I DEMAND. "CONSIDER THIS A FREE PASS. If I see you again you won't be so lucky."

"Nuh-uh," Lydia says, shaking her head. "Kiley's somewhere up there and I need to make sure she gets out of here alive. You're gonna get Hunter out of here, right? Then we're working together to get them *both* out." She purses her lips and narrows her eyes. "Then it's game on."

I roll my eyes but do not argue. Another blast shakes the compound, felt even this far underground and Hunter's eyes widen.

"We have to go!"

I grab him by the arm to drag him behind me when he stops and pulls his arm free.

"We can't leave Ismae."

"I don't have keys for that," Lydia says, checking the key ring she was given earlier. "And there's no *way* we can carry that unless you're a lot stronger than you look," she says, directing the last statement at me. I shake my head no.

"I'll come back for Ismae. We'll go find Kiley, and *you'll* run, like we agreed," I say, directed at Lydia. "Then I'll get them settled with a safe way out of here, and I'll come back for her. She should be in the possession of the Keepers anyway."

Lydia opens her mouth, but instead of speaking she purses her lips. I raise my eyebrows in challenge, knowing it's unlikely she has a better plan unless that plan is to find Victor—which is the part of my plan that I left out.

"It's a burial vault," Hunter offers. "It's reinforced with steel rebar but I doubt it could survive an explosion."

Lydia and I both look at him with surprise, but another sound added to the choir of chaos above distracts us: a helicopter. We dart for the stairs, Lydia pushing the door shut behind us but not locking it.

"Are they looking for her?" she demands as we dash up the stairs.

"I have no idea." I shake my head, cresting the stairs. At the top I hang back a moment, listening before elaborating. "I had no idea they were going to move in like this."

"How did you not know? You were infiltrating for the Keepers, right?" Her question is more a statement: no malice behind it, just curiosity.

"Not—sort of? I wasn't in contact with the Council. I haven't been since I got here."

She doesn't ask a follow-up question, instead pulls the door open a crack and jerks her head towards the back of the house.

"Come on!" she whisper-shouts, tugging the door open and slinking around the corner, her back hugging the wall. "It's a clear shot to the back door, but we won't know what's inside until we get there."

Along the horizon are flashes of light and rumbling—lightning and thunder. A helicopter above, the wind. The storm centered here, on Project Harvest. But is Project Harvest the eye of the storm, or am I? I think to the chain of events this night that have led me here: Victor telling me to leave, my refusing. Pierce intercepting him, as he has with increasing frequency these past few nights, always in the right place at the wrong time. Victor sending me to the cellar with Lydia—Lydia who seems to have as close a bond to Ismae, at least by her reputation, as I do by Blood. Lydia who cares enough for Kiley to wade into the fray to find her friend, working with *me*, no less. Lydia who could go out fighting right now, and maybe even take me down with her, but does not. I side-eye her as we run, Hunter between us.

There are no lights in the windows as we make

our way towards the rear of the house to a back entrance. Either the Praedari killed the power to give themselves advantage over the Keepers' ground troops, or the Keepers took out their power as a scare tactic. Dread turns my stomach at what the latter might mean, the Keepers likely unaware of the rows and rows of sleeping mortals donating their time and blood, vulnerable to whatever unfolds around them. Unless someone's been communicating with them about the Project. Unless someone else here has loyalty to the Keepers, but I can't dwell on that as Lydia leads us inside.

"Shoot, Hunter—you can't see," I say, but in the darkness his hand swats my arm as he waves us off.

"Give me a moment to let my eyes adjust. I've always had better-than-average night vision, plus there's ambient light from outside," Hunter says.

Lydia creeps ahead, opening a door a crack and then waving us to follow. We listen to the din of shouting and footsteps and the crackle of gunfire, the rumbling closer now as warning shots turn lethal. If Kiley's still in here I hope she stayed in her room waiting for rescue.

"They're in the main part of the facility, I think," Lydia offers, leading us down halls. "Probably sent by Victor to defend the tanks. They have extra security measures down that way in case of a breach, some chemical weapons and stuff."

"Will it reach us?"

She doesn't answer, just leads us down twisting hallways. I notice we've gone in a loop and are again at the meeting place of three hallways. I'm about to question her when her voice cuts through the relative silence.

"Kiley!" Lydia runs for the girl, arms open, meeting her in a tight hug.

Kiley clutches her duffel bag and a makeshift wooden stake carved from something shiny, a piece of furniture, perhaps? I wonder how she got it but Hunter's voice startles me, shrill.

"Delilah!" I spin on my heels and he's being shoved into me by a Praedari I recognize but cannot name. Blood seems to hang in the air between Hunter and the Praedari, as if time has stopped but of course it hasn't and Hunter slumps to the ground, twitching, something protruding from his chest. Wood.

Lydia hisses and dives between the Praedari and Kiley who steps back to cower against a wall. She has a shaft of wood in her hand, but holds it awkwardly, like one might hold a bowling ball down by her side. Lydia plucks it from her hand and charges the Praedari.

I follow Hunter to the floor, pressing my hand to his chest around the stake to staunch the bleeding. He sputters and groans, eyes wide. Blood pools underneath him and I pull him onto my lap.

"Hunter! Hunter, can you hear me?"

"Wake her," he manages to whisper, and I think I've misheard so I ask again: "Hunter?"

His breath comes ragged, sputtering. The stake pierced his lung, I would bet. He whispers "Wake her, Del—"

"Hunter. Hunter, I can save you. I can make you—"

But he jerks his head, an approximation of a shake. "Wake—"

The choking stillness that follows a final breath never leaves you, the way the body slumps once life has gone. I cradle his torso in my lap. I offered to make him an Everlasting. Why didn't he accept? It is different when they ash, a sunburst of powdery gray-white and a smear of blood. I hear Kiley screaming the same syllables again and again, Lydia pulling her tight in consolation over the pile of ash that killed the boy. The pile of ash that lunged for *me*, but found Hunter instead.

వ్రా

Dear reader, in that moment I wanted to ask *why* because that's what you're supposed to do in that moment, but I could not. Because I *knew* why:

soaked in his Heartsblood, I watched Hunter take his final breath—just as Ismae asked of me.

5

Now

I T'S NOT UNTIL THE SECOND OR THIRD RUMBLE THAT Victor looks up from the paperwork he stares at. He sits at his desk in the office of the medical portion of the facility, file folders labeled Hunter and Kiley and Logan and Charlie stacked before him, each stuffed to bursting with scraps of paper. *How could we have been so wrong?* he thinks. All this careful research, hours upon hours of manpower. Tracking them down, hours more. Capturing them, hours more. Housing them here against their will, unnecessary stress for them, for the staff of the facility, for him. He shrugs to himself.

He eyes the manila folder Pierce delivered to him, the contents the translation of the ritual to awaken Ismae the Bloody, marked in places with bright orange Post-Its and in others with neon pink or a comparatively dull purple—corrections, notes, possible alternate translations. Some intel stolen from the Keepers, some provided by Praedari scholars. Really, the ritual belongs to neither sect, the practice predating both, but when has that stopped a turf war? Praedari hid their notes from the Keepers, and vice versa. How much time has been wasted translating what the other already had?

At first he thinks it thunder, how it rolls through the far-off mountains, but the way it sounds from a single location and moves closer catches his interest. Not thunder, some kind of explosion? Victor stands, stretches his arms upwards, clasping them above his head with a grunt. He just learned of the change in the ritual when he sent Lydia and Delilah to the cellar and he fully intended to join them as he'd promised, but he wanted to make sure their remaining guests were released, or offered release, as soon as possible. He'd be lying if he didn't admit that he also wanted to give Lydia time to deliver the news herself to Hunter.

Hunter. Victor sighs, rubbing his brow. The one they'd wronged perhaps the most—not that Charlie had an easy time. Were it not for Doctor Larkin, she wouldn't be alive, much less *enhanced* as she was which probably aided in her and Logan's escape. But still, Hunter bore the brunt of their punishment when Victor made an example of him by sending him to the cellar for solitary confinement.

Only a few days passed and he was fed and kept hydrated—but it's the first time Victor saw their plight as imprisonment and it didn't sit well with him. He planned to move Hunter back in with Kiley in a few days, then Pierce brought him the updated translation of the ritual.

Another rumble and Victor heads for the door leading into the hallway. It whooshes open, bringing with it the chaos of people running, shouting to one another. In the direction of the tanks he sees his medical team in varying states of confusion, his head physician, Doctor Larkin, just looking up from his clipboard and catching his eye, giving a wave and a smile before his assistant, Doctor Amel, touches his elbow, pointing towards the chaos Victor found himself greeted with.

"Victor!" A man in outdated, faded Air Force garb strides towards him, his olive-tan leather combat boots squeaking on the tile. His nametag says *Greiner*, his insignia denoting Rank 06 or so—Lieutenant Colonel? Colonel? Victor can't remember. "The guard shacks have reported the aerial assaults are getting closer. They think the purpose of them is to distract us, or to make our terrain difficult to navigate for those trying to flee."

Victor frowns, frustrated with himself for not noticing the anomaly earlier, having attributed it to thunder in his reverie. "Do we have any idea who's behind it?"

"Nothing confirmed, but odds are it's the

Keepers—whether directly or pulling strings in the mortal world."

"We have contingencies in place, right? And they've been initiated?"

"Not much we can do until we see ground vehicles or cavalry, but the facility's being put on lockdown, starting here in the medical bay."

The rest of Greiner's explanation is mostly drowned out by an explosion much nearer than the rest. Internal alarms trigger with a wail, red-and-white lights flashing in the hallway where they stand and everywhere in their field of vision.

Ahead, the medical team busies themselves with the protocol they've practiced weekly but never had to enact in a real emergency. Nameless white-coated staff punch buttons. Layers of translucent, bullet-proof material extend from the ceiling and floor, meeting at the center in a diagonal. The last Victor and Greiner can see before their line of sight cuts off is a similar door coming together at a diagonal center seam. This barrier between them and the medical wing of the facility is built of a proprietary compound, some steel alloy his team developed, capable of withstanding more of a blast than other things on the market.

"That sounded like a hit!" Victor exclaims, but Greiner is already shouting something to the person on the other end of a radio that was clipped at his hip.

"We've been hit! A tank took out the garage. Helicopter now onsite," he reports before shouting again into the radio. "Why am I *just* hearing about a tank?!"

Both men turn their attention in the other direction, the telltale *whish* of the sector's electricity being pulled, grid-by-grid, until the hall darkens— one of the fail-safes put into place in anticipation of enemy invasion, in an effort to slow them down should they have already breached, or discourage them from doing so if they hadn't yet.

"Why the garage?"

"Maybe they don't know *where* to strike since

they don't have intel on the inside? Or, if they *do* know, maybe they don't want to take out the labs?" Greiner looks at Victor, awaiting instructions. "What do we do, Boss? Funnel everyone onsite into the labs and fight from there if we have to?"

"How long until our backup arrives?"

"Hard to say," Greiner admits. "This escalated more quickly than our drills prepared us for."

Victor shakes his head. "Then no. That means opening back up and the donors will be vulnerable while we organize. We're too spread out for that."

"We've got vehicles on the move, Boss. They've commandeered some of ours and are coming in with their own. They've got more tanks, just breaching the perimeter of the property line!"

"Finish lockdown, then coordinate with your men to get as many of our people off-site as possible. Core personnel only on the outside while we wait for our backup. They won't be long," Victor instructs before sprinting down the hall towards the farmhouse.

He navigates a series of hallways towards the quiet back entrance. He opens the door a crack, peering out to confirm the path is clear before darting outside, back pressed against the side of the building as he picks his way to the cellar. Of all the places he could've unwittingly sent her, Delilah is probably safest there within the stone walls of the unassuming storm cellar. But should the Keepers make it that far onto the property, her and Lydia could easily find themselves cornered with no choice but to fight. Not to mention that if the Keepers are looking to rescue their own, Delilah's presence there in the cellar would lead them directly to Ismae the Bloody.

Heaving open the outer door to the cellar, Victor slips down the stone stairs, pausing to listen at the door. Silence. He pushes it open—unlocked. No sign of life, save for the burial vault, chains still intact. No sign of life, but no sign of struggle either. Lydia must've brought them up to the facility— maybe to collect Kiley, to find him, or to hop into a truck and flee. The reason doesn't matter. Victor knows that he must find them before the Keepers do, and preferably before they find a way off the property.

He sprints up the stairs, the door of the storm cellar clanging behind him as he bursts into the night. He starts for the back entrance that he crept out of but hears commotion within, so he re-routes, coming up alongside the darkened farm-house towards the destroyed garage. There he stops, pressing himself against the side of the farmhouse, inching forward.

Victor doesn't hear anyone come up behind him, and doesn't see anyone lurking in shadows alongside the farmhouse. Nothing, until he feels a needle-like jab in his neck, and his veins turn to fire. His voice sounds as if underwater and he's not sure whether the shadowy figure in front of him can hear him or if his voice is caught in the fire inside him, burnt away forever, char as the rough of gravel embeds itself superficially into the flesh of his face, sticking in the blood of his broken nose and split lip.

6

Now

"HELP ME," I STAND, LAYING HUNTER'S BODY gently to the side. His eyes closed as he sputtered and shook on my lap, a small blessing I realize as I catch Kiley staring down at him. "Help me awaken her."

Lydia nods. "I have the keys we need."

"You said you didn't!"

"I lied," she states plainly. "Do you *really* want to argue the ethics of that right now?" Though her words are feisty, they lack the punch she usually delivers. Her eyes linger on Hunter a moment before she speaks again. "I wasn't going to run just because you told me to—I was going back for her. You thought I was going to let the Mother of the Praedari go home with the Keepers?"

"Shut up, shut up, shut up, shut up!" Kiley screams, shoving Lydia away from her. "He's dead! He's dead and *you're* not and you should be!"

Kiley lunges for me, pummeling me with fists, sobbing. I'm pinned against the wall, a punching bag for her grief. She only lasts a minute or so before collapsing. I catch her.

"Kiley, this is the last thing Hunter said to me. He wants me to awaken her. It doesn't matter what I think about it, or what Lydia thinks about it. This is what he wanted."

She nods, wiping tears from her eyes though they keep coming. "Why?"

I don't have an answer for her that she would understand, so I just repeat myself: "It's what he wanted."

I lead us down the halls the way we came, taking point while Lydia guards Kiley from behind. There is shouting ahead, and gunfire, so I spin, catching Kiley by the waist and shoving her into a run with Lydia now in the lead. Lydia and I communicate wordlessly with head jerks and pointing, hand to our ear if we hear something the other does not, finger to nose if we catch the scent of something. We're cut off from the back entrance, but Lydia motions for the front.

"Here," she says, tossing me the keys. "You unlock her. You can probably manage the top of the vault, right?" I nod. "Me and Kiley will grab a truck and look for Victor. We shouldn't do the ritual here. We can grab Victor on our way off the property. By the time you get Ismae to the cellar door we should be able to meet you."

The front door is wide open—something of a metaphor for these past few days if I think of it in retrospect. But here, now, just a gaping hole looking out into the grass of the yard and the gravel of the driveway. I hear the crunching of shoes on the tiny sharp rocks before they come into my line of sight. Two are dragging a third. I sniff the air from instinct, but only the sour of sulfur cuts through the smoke that chokes the night around us.

I should have smelled it: the blood messing his face up from a split lip, a broken nose.

"Victor!" My voice cuts through the quiet between explosions, my body between the girls and his body for just a moment before I rush towards the two someones dragging him. They do not notice, or do not care to, and hoist him up into the open back end of a waiting van. I feel the cool of wall against my palm as I collapse, my knees finding the hard tile as I slump to the floor.

He does not kick. Does not shout. Does not fight, does not run. Does not. I cannot even sense the thing within him that should snarl and snap its jaw. Instead, there is only stillness as he lands in a pile of others likewise subdued in the back of a white van, limp as a bloodied rag doll.

He is not yet ash, but in him all I see is ash: powdery soft and light gray, light gray like his eyes. The someones turn to me and pull me to my feet. One says my name. I stare, a haze separating me from them. Smoke from the fires, or a veil. They shout but I do not hear their words. I only know they shout because of how their arms gesture, how wide their mouths open with each syllable.

"Zeke! Zeke!" I scream, but I am lost in a memory—lunging for where I once saw a pile of someones, but now see wet pavement, dumpster, hear the *caw-caw* of a raven, smell urine-soaked rags. I'm snatched by an arm around my waist and caught off balance, falling into the sturdy trunk of someone.

"Not Zeke," I hear and I shake my head. Of course not Zeke. Victor, Victor in the back of a van, not moving but not dead because not ash.

"No, not Zeke—but—Kiley!" I turn my head, looking for her where we'd just stood inside the hole but not finding her.

7

Now

LYDIA GRABS KILEY BY THE ARM, HARD, AND PULLS her into a hallway from the direction they'd just run from.

"Lydia!" she shrieks, tucking her arm to her chest to cradle it protectively.

"Sorry, c'mon," Lydia pleads, anticipating her friend's resistance and indicating farther down the hall with a jerk of her head.

"But Delilah's—"

"And she'll go get Ismae, and then . . . I—I don't know . . . " Lydia bites her lip. "I just know I want us to get out of here alive. Well . . . you know what

I mean. Not like Victor back there." She indicates with a jerk of her thumb behind her where she had seen him being dragged. "Let's get a truck and meet her like we agreed, okay?"

The sound of a throat clearing from behind her startles them. Lydia spins to meet the intruder face-on. There, between where they were heading and this hallway they just ducked into, her pack-mate grins, the calm of his stance disarming against the chaos behind him. Pierce takes a few steps towards them, his arms out in front of him.

"Pierce!" Lydia screeches, running at him and jumping into outstretched arms.

His strong arms are around her except it's not a hug she's met with. His welcoming smile turns to a sneer as he tears her from him by one hand in a single swift movement, as if she were a tick embedded in the skin of its victim. Bruises fingerprint where the sleeve of her t-shirt ends, and her arm is freed from its socket with a sickening pop and another screech. Pierce spins her so her back is to him, and holds her in a headlock with the crook of an elbow. She struggles, flailing against the trunk of his torso, hands grabbing at his forearm, nails digging into the flesh there.

"Hey! What gives? My arm! Pierce—" she growls. With a moment's concentration there is a pop-sucking sound and Lydia's arm is once again back in socket, though sore.

"Sorry, love—it's business."

"Pierce! Quit playing! We have to get out of here—" She growls again, jabbing with a foot behind her to kick him in the shin.

"—or the Keepers will catch us!" he mocks, punctuating the end of her sentence with a scoff.

"Yes?" Lydia shakes her head, looking at Kiley with furrowed brow a second before continuing. "Yeah . . . the whole project . . . they got Victor!"

"I'm gonna stop you right there, love," Pierce says, dragging her towards the doorway they'd ducked into this hall to hide from. "Because our ride is waiting."

"Great! Come on, Kiley . . . " But even she can hear the fall of her inflection as Pierce's grip on her does not soften.

"Oh, no—the Council has other plans for her."

"The Council?" If Lydia still had the need to swallow, she would gulp. A sinking feeling starts as a familiar spark in her gut, then spreads like wildfire fed by wind as her predator within bounds from the recesses of her psyche, eyes ablaze.

Outside, a white van waits. The same van that they drove Hunter, Logan, and Kiley—where had Kiley gone?—to the ranch, it yawns open now, a mess of arms and legs and heads there in the dark, still. Among them she makes out Victor, face bloodied, eyes closed.

She feels a small sharp pain in her neck, a split second of annoyance followed by an intense burning. Wildfire. Wildfire in her gut. Wildfire in her neck. She screws her face up in a howl but the sound doesn't see freedom before the darkness settles into her field of vision. The black char that spirals up from flame.

Then Pierce's voice is like silk in her ear: "Temperance sends her love."

Wildfire in her veins, then nothing.

8

Before

"My little wildfire, changing direction whenever the wind blows," Temperance coos.

Lydia snarls, her back against the thin metal rails of the fire escape. Below them, the city: streets alight with the bouncing headlights of cars zipping from place to place and neon signs yelling into the not-so-dark of night, laughter and crying and music and bits of conversation punctuated by angry honking, the smell of fried egg rolls and car exhaust and spilt liquor wafting upwards. She thought she'd gotten far enough from Temperance's haunts to slip away unnoticed but she'd forgotten just how far her Usher's territory sprawled, or at least her influence.

For the most part Temperance respected the preferences of her Childe, only summoning her to her side for events when she wished to show off her star pupil, her favored Childe, the most prized of her collection. Lydia sucked it up, and let Temperance dress her and introduce her to other Keepers whose names and faces and every single inane exchange of pleasantries her brain cataloged.

"Just let me leave, Temperance," Lydia warns. "It'll be easier for both of us."

"You're going with them, aren't you?" Temperance sighs. "Do you know what will happen to me if the Council finds me after you've gone?" She takes a step towards Lydia her hands in front of her as if offering her something.

"They'll kill you," Lydia shrugs. "They might not have if you hadn't come after me, but now they'll smell me on you—they'll know we spoke and that I got away."

"I hadn't intended to harm you, my Childe," Temperance reassures her. "Nor did *I* intend to bleed. I merely wished to see if I could change your mind."

"You can't," Lydia spits.

"What can they offer you that I have not? That I could not?"

"Do you want to save me from them or save yourself from the punishment of my defecting?" Lydia asks.

Temperance crinkles her nose at the accusation. "Surely you do not think me such the villain?"

Her words drip with the saccharine sweetness of the Blood they share, that which Lydia knows too well, has seen ply the wills of so many others, both Everlasting and mortal. She glares, feeling the unnamed thing within her stirring.

"Don't," she warns with a growl.

"I wouldn't dare!" she lies. "I know you've steeled yourself against the Gifts of our Blood—but I wonder, Childe, at what cost?"

"So now you're *worried* about me?"

"Of course I am!" she says, her right hand going to her chest to rest where once her heart beat for emphasis. "And I know you've been in contact with them, that they've offered you the safety and protection of a pack. That—what's his name? Johnny?" She pauses just a moment, studying her. "I see what you see in him—"

"What?! No, it's not like—"

Temperance gives a soft laugh that tinkles on the wind, making her seem both ethereal and omnipresent at the same time. "Hush now, Childe. I merely mean that his charm is in his simplicity. He's all face value. He's . . . as different from me as one could hope to find. Am I wrong, Lydia?"

Lydia glares again.

"Of course I'm not wrong. And that frustrates you."

"Just stop it, Temperance. I'm leaving. I've never fit into your world."

"As opposed to what? The life I saved you from?"

"I'll never fit into your world. If I haven't yet, I never will."

"So you're—what? The petulant teenager running away from home because you're mad at mommy?"

"This isn't about you. Not everything is about you. I'm not leaving *you*, I'm leaving the Keepers. All this 'hide from the mortal world' stuff? It's worked out well for you, you have everything, but me? I play your adoring Childe whenever you ask— and I've met some of those other Keepers a dozen times and they don't remember me."

"Please, Lydia—you've *never* played my adoring Childe, nor have I asked it of you."

Lydia shrugs, kicking the rail. "Yeah, fine. I'm just done with it, okay? Are you going to try to kill me, or what?"

"What do you think you're going to find with the Praedari, Lydia? Respect? Adoration? Belonging . . . ?" She tilts her head up and inhales deeply, a habit of the living she rarely indulges in, save for emphasis. "Belonging. You miss Aurelie. I understand why you did it: so rare that we love like a sister someone that we're in such fierce competition with. You did what had to be done."

"I don't want to fight you, but I will," Lydia threatens, fighting to keep her voice as full of resolve as her words. "And I don't think I'll win, but I'll try."

"I do not doubt that, Childe," Temperance says with a sigh. "On either count. Never have you feared death." She studies the girl a moment, cocking her head to the side. "Go."

"Go?"

"Go. Before I change my mind."

Lydia doesn't hesitate. She flips herself over the railing of the fire escape to the stairs a floor below, her Converse banging on the metal as she runs down them before her Usher can change her mind, the clanging of the stairs echoing out over the din of night.

A LONG TIME AGO, AN **SMS** LYDIA WILL NEVER know about: I've marked her. Find her.

Now

KILEY DASHES DOWN THE TWISTING HALLWAYS, finding herself darting between confused people who don't bother grabbing at her—she's just a kid, after all.

The rumor of the mistranslation has reached the ears of most of them, she figures, or they're more concerned about the assault than they are about some mortal girl with an escape fantasy. Is it escape if no one's stopping you? Spotting a doorway, she sprints through it, not really paying attention to what she's bursting into: the Praedari aren't bothering with her and aren't the Keepers here to rescue her?

Outside, she gulps fresh air as she continues running. Her sneakers crunch on the gravel but she doesn't bother with stealth as she makes her way towards the section of driveway nearer the big toolshed.

This is where Charlie and Logan once reported they had trucks and vans parked. She sees two, a van and a truck with a closed bed, and she guesses this must be where they meant. Perhaps the rest of the vehicles were already grabbed by fleeing Praedari. She peers in the door of a truck, and notices the dangling keys in the ignition before she hops in and starts the engine.

She reverses in what she thinks to be the direction of the storm cellar, recalling the map that Hunter and Charlie and Logan drafted of the facility grounds. The map they'd spent hours committing to memory, just as they did the map they drafted of the inside of the facility.

Just when she thinks she's missed it, the cellar door bursts open.

Now

I WAVE HER DOWN AND KILEY STOMPS ON THE brakes. We exchange no words while loading the mummified corpse of a small woman into the closed truck bed. Kiley regards Ismae cautiously, for a split second hesitating, as if afraid the bone might crumble to ash with her touch. I would prefer Ismae to be in her coffin, at least wrapped in a blanket and not so vulnerable, but I figure she's survived far worse than a bumpy ride in a dirty truck bed. I slam shut the tailgate, turning to the girl.

"Where's Lydia?"

Kiley bites her lip, tears forming in her eyes.

I motion for the cab of the truck and hop inside, shifting out of park.

"Talk while I drive," I say. Before Kiley can buckle her seat belt I punch the gas, sending gravel flying up behind us.

"Pierce grabbed her," Kiley explains.

"So she's going with him? Did she tell him I'm taking Ismae? What's the plan?" My questions come as a deluge, my mind immediately on to what's next and where we're going and what we might find there.

Kiley takes a deep breath. "Pierce *caught* her. I didn't stick around to see what he did with her, but he's one of *them*, I think. He dragged her towards that van, the one with Victor. I didn't stick around to see, but—" The words rush from her, escaping just short of the frantic gulping of breath of hyperventilation.

I hit the steering wheel, cussing, causing the horn to bark. Kiley jumps in the seat next to me, tears streaming down her face as she's silenced.

"Hey!" I hush her unconvincingly from clenched jaw, so unaccustomed to the emotional outbursts of mortals. My own, sure—usually ending in something breaking. "It's okay! She's not dead," I offer with a frown.

"She's not?" And for a moment I've forgotten how quickly a mortal grabs for hope when it's the only life raft offered.

I consider how much sugar to roll this explanation in, not sure how fragile her emotional state. "No, she's not. Victor, he's not, either—everyone in that van's alive. Or *at least* not dead-dead. We turn to ash when we die. They still had bodies." I shrug.

Kiley nods, choking back a sob.

"And those were Keepers. *My* kind of vampire, the good guys," I oversimplify, not even sure I believe it at this point, at least not in such simplified terms.

I glance in time to see Kiley raise an eyebrow at me, skeptical, and it's in that split second that something steps into the road. She had just managed to come back with "I don't think you're right about that," when her words turn to shrieking and pointing. My attention snaps forward again and I jerk the wheel to the left, swerving to narrowly avoid a small dark figure hopping in the road.

I purse my lips, studying the road we careen down, no real destination in mind.

"I mean, she's a Praedari. If the Keepers have her, that won't be good, right?" Kiley asks after some silence.

"She'll be put on trial. The Keepers are fair, but for most of them the outcome won't be good," I answer carefully. "Perhaps Victor especially. But if any of them were coerced or forced to assist, it's likely they'll be absolved." I pause, my tongue lingering over that last syllable: absolved, as if they committed a sin, as if the Keepers alone bear holy right to forgive that sin. I find myself questioning the truthfulness of this statement before continuing. "It was Pierce that caught her, you said? Are you sure?"

Kiley nods. "Sure. He's her packmate. We all know Pierce."

"A Keeper must've paid him off, or threatened him, or he's playing along to get the two of them out of there," I offer.

She brightens at that, not a smile but something in her eyes, not her usual Kiley-perkiness I've come to know but a little better, given the circumstances. Maybe the girl won't lose two close friends in one night. Elder Keepers would say we lose the ability to truly grieve or love or feel much of anything as we face our Becoming, that those who survive that transition transcend the need for these emotions. But they've forgotten the true power of humanity: hope. They forget this because they've been so long removed from the company of those they're sworn to protect; younger Keepers hide these traces of their mortality for fear of being called soft, or worse.

Let the girl think she might yet see her friend. Let hope rise in her like the bubbles in a pot of boiling water. Let her think her friend was betrayed by someone who was bought off only because his life was hanging in the balance, or let her think the loyalty of a pack, of friendship, absolute. Let her hang on until I can return her to her family and she can put all of this behind her.

Or he's been infiltrating Project Harvest for the Keepers. But I do not say it. I *cannot* say it, cannot stomach what it means that maybe he's been here all along with the Council's blessing and they sent me into the fray unaware. Was I sent here as sacrifice?

Now

MANY MILES OF PAVEMENT PASS UNDERNEATH them; many a roadkill lies still in the road or in the ditches, some an indiscernible mash of fur and guts, some still intact. Many songs on the radio play and have a chance to repeat once, twice, more times; and many minutes of silence pass between them when they've grown tired of the radio. They take turns driving, the other two napping or staring out the window.

Sometimes they chat, though never for too long before the topic turns grim: Morgeaux's escape, Charlie's near-death, life at the ranch. For a while, talking about Before It All seems safe, but that devolves into why Morgeaux worked nights in that neighborhood, Charlie worrying about Old Grady's fences, how lonely Logan's stepmother gets when his father works late. For a while, talking about What Comes After seems safe, but that turns to What Might Not Be There Anymore. Then silence.

On the horizon, visible suddenly as they crest a small hill, is chaos: men and women in uniform, some varying slightly from one another by jurisdiction or rank, and some not in uniform but gesturing and speaking into two-way radios with sidearms at their hips—all scrambling, trotting, sweeping past one another, enveloped in whatever task they've been assigned. Most of their uniforms are still neatly pressed, free of ash or debris or dirt, or anything to suggest the destruction at what that reporter called Ground Zero.

Huddled around a large map, four non-uniformed people point and gesture, a source of light on the ground between them. One of them speaks into a radio clipped at her shoulder. They do not wear uniforms, but they wear the rank of military officers of various grades. Two of them hold white paper coffee cups nearly as tall as their heads. One of them laughs.

Back here it is a quieter chaos, a safer chaos, the chaos of orchestrating rather than enacting. Not crowd control—the only civilians Morgeaux, Charlie, and Logan see are themselves and the few reporters who now cower behind the cordon rather than report from inside the property line— but calling the shots and securing the perimeter. Cleaning up.

"We're coming up on the police cordon—who do we talk to?" Morgeaux asks.

"Maybe it's done. Maybe they got everyone out," Logan suggests as they roll up to the gathering of officers.

One officer pulls away from the swarm and approaches, flashlight shining into the windshield forcing Morgeaux to shield her eyes. His hand on his pistol, ready. Morgeaux stops the truck a few yards away and rolls down her window.

"Ma'am, this is a secure area. I'm going to need you to pull over there," he commands with a gesture to the shallow ditch between road and pasture.

Another officer approaches, sidling up to the passenger side to Logan's already open window, essentially blocking Morgeaux's ability to pull off the road if she had wanted to. "You kids can't be here. It's not safe. And it's after curfew," he barks, peering into the truck at the three.

"There are prisoners in there!" Charlie shouts to the first man from her spot in the backseat.

Morgeaux glares at her a moment, then returns her gaze to the officer. "Yes, two teenagers. A skinny boy and a girl with wild hair—"

That's when the valley beyond the security cordon lights up, the rumble immediately following. Have you ever heard someone describe the sound of a gun firing? People are always mistaking a car backfiring or someone playing with fireworks down the street as shots ringing out, so they call 911. But when it's actual gunfire they don't recognize it as such. Sometimes actual shots being fired go unreported.

They feel the truck shudder with the force of the blast and each inhales sharply, looking to the other two. Charlie darts from the vehicle first, followed closely by Logan who has to round the front of the vehicle to join her. His door knocks into the second officer who greeted them but he merely steps back and lets Logan pass. Morgeaux opens her door, steps out. The first officer is already following Charlie and Logan to where, in a moment, they'll all five stand to gaze out over the blaze.

You would expect more fire, perhaps, everything drowned in flame—and indeed, some flames rage down in the valley and swallow up parts of the buildings below. The toolshed, engulfed in flames. The silo still untouched, looming. A lot of the structure smolders, collapsed debris blocking view of the flames though they burn from within the collapse. Rarely does an explosion occur in isolation, though. A vehicle near the toolshed catches fire, gas tank erupting. Somewhere within the smolder and collapse another series of small explosions ripple.

But what they can't look away from: the part of Project Harvest that burns like aurora borealis, with swirls of color none of the three have seen as part of fire before. Charlie drops to her knees, retching, wet chunks of road trip food heaving up onto the dew-covered grass, the muffled splash of regurgitated coffee. The "back half" of the facility was where she had spent several days and nights in a fugue state being pumped full of their Blood. More than half, really, an expanse that dwarfed the attached ranch house, even the ranch house combined with all the outlying buildings. Somehow it always looked smaller from the outside. She swears she can smell burning flesh, the acrid stink of burnt hair, even though her heightened senses couldn't sort through the smoke and fire were she down there, much less way up here, above it all. Charlie doesn't remember eating this much as she keeps heaving, somehow her stomach finding more and more debris to send out of her.

Voices above her, someone laughs. *Whoooo-eeeee! Look at those colors!* And *Shut up! Shut up! Do you know what was in there? How many people they had locked up? What about all of them?* But she's not sure if she just thinks it or if she screams it and she's not sure anyone would listen to her anyway.

"What about our friends?" Charlie demands of the officer as Logan pulls her to her feet, steadying her.

"Charlie . . ." he warns in a low whisper.

"Let me stop you right there, blondie—no one was *ambul-atory* before that explosion, that's why we got the okay for the Boom Squad over there to hit the big button," he says, pointing, a strange inflection on the word *ambulatory*, as if he's repeating something he's not certain the definition of. The four assembled around the map wave and cheer, clap one another on the back, and high-five.

"And if we were wrong about that, well, there's *definitely* no one walking outta there now."

"Wait, wild hair, you said?" The second officer joins them. "Was she like fifteen or sixteen? Around your age?"

Charlie nods.

"She and a woman left in a truck." The first officer catches his eye, an exchange that doesn't go unnoticed by Charlie. "What? I was takin' a leak. Crazy broad almost hit me dodging some bird or something!"

"Which way did they go?" Morgeaux asks.

"That way," he points. "But that was a couple hours ago."

The first officer steps towards them. "It seems like you kids knew a bit about what's inside, or *who's* inside," he accuses. "I think it's best you come with me for questioning. Besides," he adds, narrowing his eyes. "It's past curfew."

Logan has already begun leading Charlie to the truck, hovering at the rear driver's side door.

Charlie scoots inside, across the seat to the passenger side, leaving room for him.

"Of course, officer," he says, smiling. "We'd be happy to."

Morgeaux strides to the driver's side, door still open, she hadn't bothered closing it. She echoes Logan's smile with her own, her voice matching his eager-to-please tone. "Should we meet you at the precinct?"

The officer, still glaring, nods. "Yeah," he barks. "The precinct."

"We'll call our parents on the way," Morgeaux offers. "Doesn't a minor need a guardian present for questioning?" But it's not a question, not the way she says it.

"Yeah," the man barks again. "You can follow us."

The doors of their vehicle shut as the two officers head towards their car.

"Buckle up!" Morgeaux says, punching the gas, sending a few loose pebbles flying as the truck guns in the direction the other officer said Kiley and some woman had gone.

In the rearview mirror she sees her passengers scrambling to buckle their seatbelts and, outside, the two officers shouting and gesturing. Neither rushes to pursue them, instead the first speaks into the radio clipped at his shoulder.

"We can't outrun them," Logan states from the back seat. "And they know what this car looks like."

"Well, unless one of you has a better plan, this is it for now," she says, shrugging from the driver's seat. The other two don't offer anything. No flashing red-and-blues in sight for now, so Morgeaux drives. Shortly, she says, "If they went this way, they were probably heading for the city."

"There's probably more than one city within a few hours of here," Logan guesses.

"Yeah, but only one that matters to the vampires," Morgeaux offers. She'd heard Quinn and the others at the safehouse talking about the Keepers, about some Council of Elders that's headquartered in the arts district of the capital.

"How do you even know that? Besides, that's like nine—twelve?—hours away," Charlie protests.

"Then let's hope that I'm right, and that one of them is a vampire and they have to pull over at daybreak."

"That's a lot of things to hope," Charlie grumbles from the back seat.

Now

VICTOR COMES TO WITH A GROAN, SOMEWHERE
dark and small—not small like a coffin, but
small like a closet. There are bars between him
and more darkness, more room. Sniffing, he smells
blood long dried, his own staining his shirt. His
nose and lip have healed on their own, even without him consciously forcing the Blood, probably
something to do with whatever they injected him
with. His hand goes to his neck and he rubs. No
raised bump, nothing he can feel to prove he'd
been stabbed at all. His eyes adjusting, he scans
his surroundings: a hallway and more cells like his,

each with a dark form slumped on the ground as if dumped there. One dark figure looks familiar even in the darkness, messy hair, cut-off denim shorts, fishnets underneath, cropped leather jacket.

"Lydia!" he whispers, crawling two feet to the bars of the cell, able to see a bit more of the corridor from this vantage point but not seeing an end in either direction. "Lydia! Are you awake? Lydia?"

He pulls on the bars, straining and groaning, but they will not bend. The realization sinks into his gut: Keepers. A Keeper prison, or dungeon, bars even the Everlasting are not meant to bend. He hears someone out of his line of sight stir and then the familiar sound of footsteps shuffling in a cadence to suggest them not being bound by bars.

"Hello? Hello? Who else is here? Lydia, can you hear me?" Victor calls out, glancing down the corridor in either direction, then to her form still unresponsive in the cell across from his own.

His questions meet with the echo of laughter from down the hall. Click, step, step, click—a touch of light down the corridor. He pushes his face against the bars, straining to see further in the direction of the sound with a different angle, but cannot. Click, step, step, click—more light.

"Awake already? I'll have to let them know the dosing almost wasn't strong enough," a familiarly accented voice mocks. Click, step, step, click—this circle of light nearly touches the bars Victor clings to.

"Pierce?" The question is met with visual confirmation as Pierce steps from the shadows, clicking on a light right next to Victor's cell.

"In the flesh," he grins. "I'm not here to pay a visit, though, just here to move the girl."

Pierce turns to Lydia's cell and unlocks the door which he then heaves open with some difficulty. He grabs her roughly, hoisting her over his shoulder in a fireman's carry. The doorway isn't wide enough, though, her face smashing into the metal with a clang. Pierce winces with a laugh that rises up through the relative silence of the prison chamber.

"That'll smart when she wakes up!"

"Wait! Pierce! Wait—" Victor pleads, scrambling to his feet. "Why are you doing this? What's going on? Where are we?"

"'Tis a pity we don't have time to chat, old friend. But I'll be back for you."

"Where are you taking her? Please?" Victor's voice rises with urgency. "Pierce, please?! Lydia! Lydia! Wake up! Please!"

His cries fall away to angry, gasping sobs as he kicks the door of the cell. It clangs in place, showing no signs of give. Pierce doesn't answer, instead whistling "Ring of Fire" on his way down the corridor, the familiar tune cutting into the still air of an unfamiliar chamber—one of Victor's favorites.

Now

QUINN WATCHES FROM HER PERCH IN THE IN-BE-tween, from the shadow Asgard cast on the world. She'd glimpsed Delilah and the wild-haired girl fleeing the blood farm, the Slumbering form of Ismae the Bloody tucked into the truck bed unceremoniously, rattling around like the bunch of bones she is, and with that information she visited one of the Volur, one of the witches among the Valkyries who practiced the Old Magic, seidhr.

More than soothsayers, the Volur wield magic rather than falling victim to its whims, summoning and commanding horrific war-forms in preparation for Ragnarok. One does not seek their counsel lightly, and they always demand a price. The Valkyries counted among their ranks witches of many faiths, but none so frightening in their potential as the Volur.

This particular Volur did not demand she pay her price right there, insisting it could be paid when she called upon Quinn later—nor did she give a name by which she could be called upon, her features obscured in the oversized, but seemingly authentic skull of a raven. Her body was marked in symbols Quinn could not place. She sliced each of their palms and they shook hands—then she banished Quinn for the remainder of the night, telling her she would know the answer to her question when she was meant to, but not a moment sooner.

That magic led her here: The Seahorse Inn.

First learning to navigate Asgard took some getting used to, the shadow thick as water, a sense almost like drowning but alien enough to disarm even her, an Everlasting who hasn't needed breath in decades, or maybe longer. It's so easy to lose track of time, and how long does it take a mortal to drown, anyway? She had an easier time of it, of learning to walk the shadow, than her mortal sisters—but the other side of the coin, of course, was that there were things that came easier to the living than to the dead. Now she finds traveling through Asgard as natural as she found breathing when she was mortal.

She stands at the tailgate of the truck, studying it. She could peer beyond it to the prize inside, a trick of the shadow with just some concentration, but instead she reaches through the shadow into the waking world and unlatches the metal truck-bed cover with a touch. She does not throw it open, but brings down the tailgate in the same manner.

Shadow drips from her, forming something like wings at her back that unfurl and flap twice, stretching, then reaching forward, around her. Their feathery softness crosses the threshold into the living world easily, envelopes the fragile, mummified remains of the Slumbering Elder, drawing her tight against Quinn's body. A cocoon of darkness encasing them both. If she still drew breath, she would struggle to do so now. She closes her eyes, clenching her jaw as the wings wrap them tighter and tighter still. If she still drew breath, she would have drawn her last.

Quinn grimaces as she feels an unfamiliar pop-pop of her ribs cracking outward, as she hears the same cracking of the ribs of the Slumbering Elder echo her own in the feathery embrace. She expects a rain of bonedust down onto the pavement at her feet, expects a puff of ash in place of the Elder. She can't help but scream, lucky her screams are swallowed by layers of shadow, unable to disturb the waking world. Her rib cage opens as if hinged, opening to receive Ismae the Bloody. The wings continue to press the two of them together, only partially under her control as the magic has begun and, once begun, only a sacrifice could stop.

Come home, Ismae.

The wings feed Ismae into her, like wood into a chipper except the mummified Elder dissipates into vellum-like shadow, then shadow-web, then nothing. Quinn throws her head skyward as her eyes roll back, only the whites visible. She inhales sharply, light entering her. She swears she draws within her the moon's silvery cast, the light thrown by every star in every galaxy, the magic of starlight itself. Though she cannot see through the remaining black, she feels it fill her veins. It's as if she's not only absorbed the light, but become the dark.

There is a searing pain in the palm of her outstretched hand before a bright white shoots from it, something of a sword of light which her hand then wraps around. In her other hand is that same sear, then a shield of light forms. Though she's never fought with shield before, her body does not hesitate to take up the ancient battle stance. She exhales shadow, a ribbon following the trajectory of her breath, shaping itself into a raven which flaps its wings and lands at her feet.

Her head snaps forward and she looks down, examining her chest. Not open, not hinged. She draws in an unnecessary breath, anticipating the sharp of fractured rib but only feels full. The shadow around her once again murky, no longer opaque, as if she never inhaled all the light within a ten foot radius. In her hands no sword, no shield; no raven at her feet. Even the wings she called upon have recoiled, furled into her body once again. She would not believe any of it, were it not for one fact: Ismae was gone.

15

Now

LUCKILY THERE'S NOT MUCH BETWEEN WHERE THEY were and where they wanted to end up. Morgeaux drives an hour past daybreak, then pulls off at every town that's an upgrade from the usual podunk "two dive bars and a church" that seems to dominate the area. They pull into every motel, Charlie and Logan scanning the parking lot for one of the ranch's work trucks, the familiarity of them burned into their mind's eye like when you can't recall your license plate number but have no difficulty locating your car in a sea of others like it.

One after another, nothing. Morgeaux rubs her eye.

"Want me to drive?" Logan offers but Morgeaux shakes her head.

"Just a bit of mascara in my eye, I'm gonna pull off a sec," and she does, habit pulling her into the parking lot of The Seahorse Inn, a rundown, sprawling motel dreadfully far from sea or seahorse.

Morgeaux uses the rearview mirror to dab her eye with a tissue she wets with saliva.

"There! Good as new! Logan, can you grab me a Red Bull?"

Logan hands her a Red Bull from the white styrofoam cooler meant for bait that they bought and stocked at the beginning of this leg of the trip. Red Bulls, water, a few plastic containers of Greek yogurt. A plastic bag filled-to-bursting with Twizzlers, chips, candy, crackers, beef sticks—the basic assortment of junky road-trip food—next to him on the seat. A white paper cup of once-hot coffee occupies every cupholder in the vehicle, each empty or nearly empty by now.

"Should we just pull off for a bit and sleep?" Logan asks, casting a sidelong glance at Charlie. Her eyes bloodshot and puffy, she hasn't spoken in at least an hour, before offering few-word replies when the other two discussed their next move, now just unresponsive.

"We should keep going. If they're sleeping—"

"That's assuming that Kiley is *with* a vampire," Logan argues. "She might not be."

"But she *might* be, and that's our best bet right now. We don't really have a better plan and we're all cool with heading to the city anyway, right? Once we're there, if we haven't found her, we can try to find her family or contact the authorities there."

Logan leans back in his seat, seemingly satisfied that there's more to the plan than chasing down someone they may or may not find based on whether they are or aren't with a vampire right now.

The sprawling metropolis and its suburbs and outlying counties that they each called home before they were plucked from it by the Praedari and thrown together.

Morgeaux chugs the Red Bull, tossing the empty can to the floorboard of the front passenger seat before pulling around the side of the motel to continue their tour de parking lot.

"That's it! That's the truck!" Logan shouts, pointing to a familiar truck as they round the corner to the back of the building.

"Are you sure?" Morgeaux doubts.

"Yes! Pull up, pull up." She does, pulling up next to the truck.

Logan jumps out before she can even shift to park, his door hanging open as he circles the truck.

"This is from the ranch. Here, see this truck cover? If you open it—" Logan explains as he fidgets with the latch to open the hardcover of the truck bed which has warmed with morning sun.

"He's right! That's the truck with the cover that's

rusting out, with the latch that sticks," Charlie says, joining him. "Here, you know only I can get the thing open." She nudges him aside and in two deft movements starts lifting the metal truck bed cover.

"Okay! Stop messing with it though—" Morgeaux interrupts. "We have to figure out which room this truck belongs to."

"Then what?" Logan asks.

"Then we camp out."

They take turns sitting outside the door behind which Kiley sleeps, on the concrete strip of side-walk that leads up to and between the rooms, a step up from the carefully manicured lawn that stands in stark contrast to the peeling paint and cracked wooden beams of the building itself. The proprietor yelled at them that they'd have to buy a room to stay on the property, that they can't just sit outside and not pay, so they paid for the room next to where they believed Kiley to be and sleep in shifts, one sleeping and two guarding.

Charlie held out until the last shift and now steps out of the room as the sun dips just below the horizon in a beautiful display of orange and pink and purple as the bluish dusk of night comes on. The other two greet her with fingers to their lips and wave her over. She stands, ear to the door for just a second before nodding at them, the Blood within her allowing her more acute hearing to discern Kiley's voice, though muffled behind the door.

Then she hears another voice and Charlie mouths "Delilah" to the other two. Logan nods, Morgeaux offers a half-shrug and furrowed brow, not understanding. Footsteps clunk-clunk closer to the door so the three step back, creating a blockade with their bodies as the door opens.

Their breath catches in their throats, one after the other, imperceptible to anyone except Charlie, as Kiley stops in her tracks, eyes wide with surprise.

Tears well up in her eyes as she rushes Logan and throws her arms around his neck.

"Logan! Charlie!" she cries out, hugging Charlie in turn. "How did you find me?!"

Delilah steps outside behind her, mirroring her surprise.

"And you! I don't care who you are!" Kiley throws her arms around Morgeaux who just laughs and hugs her back.

"I'm Morgeaux—I think you guys call me The One That Got Away?" She smiles at Delilah. "You *helped* me get away. Thank you."

Delilah offers a smile in return.

"Did *she* kidnap you?" Charlie demands of Kiley, eyes narrowed at Delilah who rolls her eyes.

"Huh? No! No, it's a long story, but we were going to leave with Lydia and Hunter—" Her face falls. "Hunter—Hunter didn't make it," Kiley finishes softly, tears already falling. "Lydia, they took her and—"

"And Victor," Delilah offers. "Me and Kiley here made it out, not sure how many others did."

"No thanks to *you*, I'd imagine," Charlie accuses.

"Did I miss something?" Morgeaux interjects, looking from Charlie to Delilah.

"No. Delilah explained it to me," Kiley says, directing it at Charlie. "There's a lot to it you don't understand. She never meant for any of us to get hurt."

Charlie doesn't answer, just continues glaring.

"Well, we have a lot of miles to figure it all out," Logan suggests. "And we'll all fit."

"Can't," Delilah starts, but Kiley interrupts.

"Actually, two in the front, three of us in the backseat and then she can maybe ride in the back-back? Won't be any worse than that truck bed," Kiley offers, wiping tears away and taking a deep breath.

"They say we can't feel in that state, though we're aware," Delilah explains. "Not much she could say about it anyway." She shrugs.

"She?" Charlie demands.

"Come see," Kiley says, gesturing for them to follow, already leading them towards the truck.

She struggles with the latch of the truck cover a moment before Charlie steps forward and pops it, wasting no time throwing it open and out of the way. She peers inside. A pause.

"What?"

"*What* what?" Kiley asks.

"There's nothing here," Charlie explains, turning her head to look at her friend.

Delilah shoves forward through the assembled teenagers, her gaze following where Charlie's just left. She cusses, punching the tailgate to leave a dent and a smear of blood as the skin of her knuckles cracks open on impact.

"What the—?" Kiley shrieks, grabbing tightly to the top of the tailgate, knuckles whitening.

Now five sets of eyes stare into the same empty truck bed.

Now

AFTER ISMAE VANISHED, I HAD LITTLE REASON TO return to the city—except to try and figure out where the captured Praedari had been taken. The five of us drove to an abandoned park at the edge of the city, where we said our goodbyes. Now, here, waiting with Pierce for the Council to invite us into their chambers, I have a hard time believing I won't see the four of them again.

I feel Pierce's eyes on me and cast a sidelong glance in his direction. I wonder how many times he's waited here to be beckoned inside, how many times he's counted the knots in the mahogany paneling, how many times he's heard the clink-clink of the crystals in this chandelier.

How many seasons' fresh flowers has he been greeted by as they adorn small antique tables to either side of the door, welcoming. Did he notice their brightness, how the blooms mock against the grim art so carefully curated by Alistair? Had he met Alistair? And the others?

I stare at the painting that held my attention rapt when I first visited these chambers. A woman wearing bloodied tatters and covered in faint traces of Nordic tattoos, a raven headdress, all skull and feathers.

She could be Quinn, or her dead sister, were it not for her blond hair. A battlefield at night, the ground covered in freshly dead, like where I stood as Ismae in her memory.

The only things in the painting not marred by battle and blood are the sword and shield the woman holds: nothing to hint at the slaughter. Her eyes glow faintly, as does the aura around her, but this time it's the shadows I notice, not the light. The artist probably intends that our eyes fall to the wisp of light trailing from one of the corpses to the blade of her sword, but my gaze rests upon the other dead, how they've fallen to shadow or already lost their light.

Snuffed out, or taken?

"I really am sorry, love—" Pierce starts but I interrupt with a wave of my hand, dismissing his apology.

"Save it," I snap.

I'm not angry at him, not really. How could I be? He had a job to do and he was doing it, like Zeke, me, Brittany, the suicide bomber, and how many others? Knots in wood, unaware of the rest. Keeper operatives lived in a vacuum unless by chance they recognized one another, Zeke explained to me after the raid all those years ago.

Sometimes, if their assignments overlapped long enough, they'd come to notice the tells, but even then it went unspoken because you never know who's listening.

"I just mean that I would've *said* something if I could have that night in the alley," he says, turning to me. "She—Morgeaux—wasn't in any danger, not really."

"Not in any danger?" I scoff. "Please. Hunter's *dead.*"

"That's regrettable," he offers. "But it wasn't by *our* hand. Not yours or mine, at least."

"And that makes it okay?" I take a step towards him, hands balled into fists at my side. "How long have you been undercover?"

"Since Lydia left her Usher's care," he says, lips pursed and eyes narrowed in thought, but I cut him off before he can calculate the years he's spent at her side as her packmate.

"My first sip was as a Praedari," I hiss. "I clawed my way from the earthen womb that rebirthed *us*, my Praedari brothers and sisters, *me.*"

"So you're angry the blood farm fell?" he asks.

"I—I—" I stammer, afraid I've lost my momentum like I've almost certainly lost my point. "I'm *saying* that you've lived as one of them, but I was *made* as one of them. Any life lost in an operation is, as you say, *regrettable*—but when it could've been prevented? That's *messy*. That's incompetence. What's more? No remorse makes you no better than they are."

Pierce shrugs, either because he doesn't have anything to add or because my train of thought derailed so abruptly he couldn't follow my tantrum. I bite my lip and narrow my eyes, about to launch into a full-on morality tirade when the doors to Council chambers open in their silent, wide arc.

Leland stands, and I remember the first time he greeted me in this manner—his suit reminiscent of, or actually from, the 1920s, perfectly pressed; an energy about him like Gatsby, with that same too-easy smile. I cock my head slightly. I wonder, who is Leland's Daisy? On someone else the suit might look like a costume, but for Leland it's something of a second skin.

"Welcome home, Delilah," he says in a cadence to suggest it's rehearsed, each syllable drawn out just slightly. "And Pierce, always a pleasure," he adds, gesturing for us to enter ahead of him.

"Sure, mate," Pierce claps him on the shoulder with a hearty laugh as he enters, startling Leland. I bite back my own laugh as Leland clears his throat almost inaudibly and straightens his tie, remembering how he guided me into chambers the first time, his hand on my lower back as if we were familiar. Suddenly I like Pierce a little more, enjoying a moment of Leland squirming.

I face a round, gleaming mahogany table and seven high-backed leather chairs, two empty. I wonder how many times Pierce has walked into this, the lion's den?

Enoch, in his gray robes, sits at the head of the table. Alistair sits stiffly, his hands on the table in front of him, clasped—his cufflinks polished, his pocket square aqua against the neutral greige of his suit, like mud, gray peppering his hair. Were it not for detail, Alistair might be swallowed up by time, made obsolete. Usually he coordinates with Temperance but tonight she stands out in all black, a mourner from another time, a black veil obscuring her features.

My gaze lingers but I am mindful to pull it away before she notices. Evelyn, in a crisp white button-down blouse and her hair in a bun—but she's missed a button and hairs stick up all over, having escaped the confines of bobby pins, a few wisps framing her face.

Brantley's feet are propped up on the table and he leans back in his seat, fingers laced behind his head, a smirk tattooed on his face. A leather messenger bag, half open, lay on the table in front of him, a set of keys hastily dropped on top.

Pierce steps inside the room and behind the chair that's been empty every time I've visited Council chambers. He stands upright looking straight ahead, his jaw set, his feet planted firmly, his arms crossed at the wrist behind his back.

I hang back, stepping just inside the doorway, leaning just slightly against the wall behind me, crossing my arms at my chest. Leland shuts the heavy doors to the chamber before taking his designated seat nearest them. Only his seat and Enoch's at the head and the empty seat in front of Pierce seem to have assignments to them; the others fill in where they will, or so it seems from the visits I've made.

It is Leland who speaks after an expectant silence that no one else fills: "The Council would like to commend you both for your service to the sect. Your loyalty has not gone unnoticed."

"And my continued loyalty the Council has," Pierce assures, as rehearsed in speech as Leland sounds—words I recognize somewhere in memory, but in Zeke's voice.

"Pierce, your long-term infiltration of a Praedari pack garnered us the continued intel that led, in part, to a successful siege on their blood farm, Project Harvest. Because of *both* of your dedication to the sect, Project Harvest is no longer a threat. Many Praedari, including some more notable in their contribution to sect politics, are in custody and await the Ritus Cruciatus. Some mortal staff were recovered, as well, and will be *rehabilitated* so that they may re-enter mortal society. For those lives lost, restitution will be offered to their families. Thank you both."

With that, Pierce turns and goes to the door, met by Leland who throws it open as if it were no heavier than paper. *Is that it? A pat on the head and we're supposed to wait for our next set of orders?*

"Delilah, if you could stay," Leland requests quietly as I follow a couple steps behind Pierce.

I stop, surprised, and offer a half-nod before hanging back. Leland waves at Pierce before again shutting the Council doors. When he turns to me, he gestures for me to take the seat next to his that's been empty each time I've visited these chambers.

"Please, sit," he offers with a smile and I do.

"Delilah, this was Pierce's first long-term assignment and he will be rewarded—but he's expected to continue his service," Temperance explains. "I recruited him when Lydia left the sect—an unfortunate turn of circumstance, but here we are."

"Okay," I say, furrowing my brow and shaking my head slightly. "And . . . you have another task for me to undertake?" I ask, trying to fill in the blanks.

She shakes her head this time. "Not at all—Delilah, the Council would like to reward you for your past and continuing service to the Keepers, but that reward *is* continued service," she riddles, allowing a smile to break out over her lips. "You're sitting in what used to be Ezekiel Winter's seat on the Council of Keepers. Yours, if you'll have it."

I remember how her voice dripped like honey when I first met her, here in these chambers. Blood pounds in my ears, not phantom drumbeat but as real as the seat underneath me. I feel a flush rise in my cheeks, hinting at something long since dead but somehow stirred up again.

My hands find the armrests of the chair and grip, the leather sticking to the skin of my forearms. The back of the chair sticks up above my head considerably and I feel small, a child-queen in a throne she's not ready for.

I see Temperance's lips move, but do not hear what's said. Other faces mirror her enthusiasm after pausing a few too many beats, colored with their own temperament: Brantley shrugs but his smirk turns up just slightly in the other corner to flash something of a small smile; Evelyn grins, the effect unsettling as another lock of hair untwists itself from her disheveled bun and drops to rest on her shoulder; Alistair unclasps his hands to reach over and give one of mine a quick squeeze; Leland dips his head in a nod.

Only Enoch, still as stone, doesn't react.

Temperance stands, waiting for me to do the

same before addressing me further: "You have until the dark moon to make your decision, Childe."

Now

THE DOOR BARELY CLICKS SHUT BY LELAND'S HAND when he spins on his heels, snarling.

"How *dare* you?!" Brantley's feet drop to the floor with a heavy *thunk*, his chair squeaking in protest as he leans forward to pound his fists on the table. "She's not fit to rule!"

Evelyn leans back in her seat with a smirk to rival the one Brantley usually wears. "*Rule*? What is this, the fourteenth century? And what right have *you* to *rule*?"

"There's a protocol to this sort of thing, Temperance," Alistair explains, his hands still clasped in front of him, his lips pursed. "In the event of a vacancy, Council is intended—"

"She doesn't need you mansplaining the Code of Keepers," Evelyn snaps, the vulgar slang she overheard from her late apprentice, Nikolai, sneaking into her ire. "His seat has been empty long enough. We've honored his contributions to the sect, but it is time to name another to take his place."

"The Council of Keepers shall be comprised of the seven eldest Keepers in the territory," Temperance recites. After a pause: "However, the Code also states, 'It remains the privilege of the Eldest of the Council of Keepers to veto or hand down a decree, so long as it upholds the vision of the First Ones and the purpose of the Council of Keepers'," she finishes.

Five sets of eyes turn to the head of the table, the seat occupied by Enoch, the eldest among them. Several moments pass in silence.

"Whether Enoch chooses to speak on the matter or not, does not change the fact: Delilah is not an

Elder, nor even the Eldest of the Blood in our *city*. Should not we approach those that are her Elder—at a minimum, out of *respect?*" Leland interrupts, glaring at Temperance to emphasize *respect*—respect that she did not show her peers on the Council, respect she did not show Enoch, the Eldest of the Blood, respect she did not even consider paying lip service to for appearances' sake, something that rattles Leland's patience and need for decorum to the core.

Heads whip in his direction, more than one set of eyes wide at the suggestion that the feelings of some unnamed Elders—younger than the each of them—should matter more than deference to Enoch's age, but Enoch himself remains unmoving. Petty politics beneath him, he feels no need to interject: let the children quarrel. All unfolds as it must.

"I offer her what she has earned," Temperance responds.

"*Earned?* Earned by what right?" Alistair accuses, hands unclasping to allow his fingers to drum on the table. "By not getting herself killed? That's self-preservation, hardly any more commendable than when any of us go to bed at dawn rather than greeting the sun. Or perhaps she earned it by drawing out an investigation of something that we could've finished off in a matter of days?"

"In all fairness," Brantley interrupts, "that was our fault for not acting sooner."

"She did what the Council asked of her. She did not request further assistance, nor tax the Council in any way. She accepted what fate lay before her, and she did so with grace."

"She did so out of the selfish, mortal desire for closure—or revenge," Alistair retorts.

"Does that change her contribution to the siege?"

"Are you suggesting that the ends justify the means, Siren?"

"I'm not sure that that's the argument I'm making, no. I'm saying that she bought us precious time, time that allowed us to set into motion things in the mortal realm that obscured the reality of the war we find ourselves a part of. We had time to involve the FBI, SWAT, and other agencies of the federal government; to tamper with media outlets; even quell suspicion, conspiracy theories, and outrage online, for as long as that ever lasts. Not to mention the other favors we called in with local emergency personnel, medical facilities, even airlines."

The orchestration rested with the Council, but they pulled in contacts and relationships cultivated by members of their sect at large to squelch crises of all sizes around the country. The Council could claim much of the credit, but their effort would have fallen flat without the support and loyalty—taking the form of blackmailing officials and disappearing problems—that other Everlasting could lend. Rare, to see so many of their kind working together, but with stakes this high, denying the Council requested support could be seen as treason.

Silence, the command thick in the air between

each of the Council of Keepers despite no mouth uttering it.

Leland, the voice that speaks, though the words are not his: "She is right. The girl has performed as well as could be expected. " Enoch, a mountain looming over foothills, continues speaking through Leland, seemingly untaxed by the effort. "She was given a task and saw it through. Whether or not she deserves a voice on this Council is a matter for another time, but she must be closely watched for signs of dissent—far easier when yoked to the legacy of her Usher. The rage of Ismae the Bloody sings in her veins, and her time amongst the Praedari, both at her Becoming and recently, makes her a liability . . . but also an asset if we can groom her properly for the position." *Perhaps the same position Ismae the Bloody declined so long ago*, but he does not speak this.

"Have we recovered what remains of Ismae the Bloody?" Temperance asks. The same Gift of the Blood that allows her to calm one's predator within often grants her a veiled glimpse into their thoughts—if not in the literal, then in effect. Not telepathy, but an innate sense of how our heart tethers one emotion to the next, in a chain that can be followed to what's left unspoken.

"Nope," Brantley interjects. "Unless princess is hiding her in an unmarked van somewhere, I don't think we will." He leans forward. "But for real, have we considered that Delilah *does* know where her Usher's Usher is and is hiding her?"

"What would she gain from that? Surely the accolades and praise we'd heap upon her for producing the Mother of the Praedari would motivate her to cooperate," Leland suggests, again in his own voice.

"Never doubt what loyalty is forged of the Blood, Leland," Brantley sings out, the accusation hanging heavy in the air.

"You have a point in that, Brantley," Temperance starts. "But the girl's fear when she reported Ismae as missing was real." Another insight—some feelings even distance and a poor cell phone connection can't obscure.

He shrugs, putting his hands in front of him as if waving a white flag. "I'm just saying that she'd be a high-ticket item if sold to any surviving Praedari."

"Sounds like you've put some thought into this, Brantley. Should we consider your *insight* some sort of admission of guilt?" Evelyn challenges. "I thought not. Now, enough of this. We must ready ourselves for the Ritus Cruciatus. The ritual chambers have been prepared by my assistants. Does anyone have questions about their role as Inquisitor?"

Heads shake in unison, features uniform in their solemnity as if just moments ago they weren't bickering like children over a toy on the playground. Each member of the Council of Keepers rises and gathers their things, starts for the door, save for Enoch who remains. Any who blink swear they see the swell of his robes, a cocoon of gray swallowing him.

With a frown, Temperance tears from her neck the small glass vial on a chain, popping the tiny cork from its mouth and turning it upside-down, letting the contents drip onto the table. Red droplets pool: Lydia's blood. She swears she can smell her Childe, the cloying of lilacs and dank of petrichor as raindrops ping off fallen autumn leaves.

"Whomever administers her Ritus Cruciatus, bring me her ashes." She keeps her voice low so that she may also keep it steady.

"You should," Alistair suggests. "She is your Childe. It is tradition." His voice softens. "And it is your right, as her Usher."

"The Council does not want that," she warns, an edge to her voice. "For if I do, I *will* consume her Heartsblood, confession or no."

18

Now

I<small>T'S EXACTLY AS</small> I <small>LEFT IT WHICH IS EXACTLY HOW</small> I remember it: a tarp on the floor painted in my blood, the reek of it now stale, with all the furniture pushed to the sides of the room to make a clearing. The apartment Zeke and I shared, the apartment that became more mine than his as his duties summoned him elsewhere with increasing frequency, as his thirst for lore kept him from me more nights than I care to admit. If only I could've become an unknown thing, a mystery for him to chase.

When I'm too honest with myself, I know that I was another of his mysteries—and not much more.

This is where Caius coaxed from me the vision that led me to Zeke's killer. *Coaxed* too gentle a word, of course, for the crude ritual designed to force the predator within me to the surface, that she might, in all her snarling and gnashing of teeth, stumble upon whatever magic, or thread that connects me to the universe and sends the visions. *Force* appropriate, too, where my convincing Caius was concerned: no part of him wanted the burden of torturing a vision from me. He's not like me and Zeke. He doesn't fight the same impulse to dance along the edge of his mortal death again and again, nor to lead that dance for someone else.

Thick drapes cover the window, blocking any light from the outside, ambient or natural. I'd replaced much of Zeke's old furniture when I took over this apartment, some out of necessity as they fell casualty to my rage or his. One of the few pieces remaining from the first time he brought me here is the expensive ivory upholstered chair still covered with a drop cloth meant to protect it from what

Caius and I did before I left. A wooden chest stands untouched, open, boasting various blades, candles, herbs. My and Zeke's ritual chest.

Shards of splintered wood litter the floor where Caius slammed his fist on an end table not meant to withstand his strength, the memory echoed by a knock at the door that startles me from reverie. Caius enters unbidden.

Before he can even turn around fully I bound at him from across the apartment, jumping and launching myself into his already open arms. He laughs. The mangled stump of his injured hand offset by his strength, he holds me to his chest easily in a tight hug, the familiarity between us born of not knowing if we'd see one another again. This man, something of an uncle to me, if could I remember what that relationship looks like. If ever I doubted his affection for me, I doubt it not in this moment.

"They told me you'd arrived. I just got in myself." He sets me down, surveying the apartment, the mess we'd left right before I started chasing down Zeke's killer. "I figured I might find you here," he adds more gently. "What ghosts have you unearthed, Childe?"

I shake my head. "None yet."

And it's true. I've only just arrived at the apartment we used to share, but I know where Zeke kept things he didn't want found. Sometimes, after he'd think I'd fallen asleep, he would dig out his journal or a stack of papers. I could tell through slit eyes that they were old: edges stained, pages wrinkled by water damage, corners dog-eared, torn. They smelled musty, too, like they weren't well kept when he'd found them. I remember coming home to pages hanging on twine crisscrossed across the apartment, drying. I'd never bothered digging through his belongings before now—out of respect, maybe, or the conditioning born of the Binding. Or because I was afraid of what I'd find. It was his unlife's work; I accepted it as fact and left it at that. Until now.

"It's best you don't go looking," he warns. "Focus on the future. It's what Ezekiel would have wanted."

"The Council offered me his seat," I say, changing the subject.

"His seat . . . on the Council of Keepers?" Where the inflection of surprise falls, I know he knew of his dear friend's position, but not their intention of offering it to me.

"You knew he was on the Council," I accuse.

Caius nods. "Honestly, there wasn't much he kept from you. It wasn't my place to share this secret."

"Even after his Final Moment?" I challenge.

"Even after his Final Moment," he echoes, unflinching. "Will you take it?"

"I might." I shrug. "Or I could follow you into the woods, live off-the-grid. You could teach me to eat squirrels or whatever it is you do out there. Or, hey, maybe I'll run off and join the Praedari," I joke, but honestly, aren't those my options? "With all those arrests they'll be recruiting soon, right?"

He laughs. "I can't imagine you hunting down anything on more than two legs. And it would be the wrong time to change ideologies and pledge loyalty to the rabble, unless you want to witness firsthand the Ritus Cruciatus. You're tough, no doubt, but not *that* tough. Enoch himself would be lucky to survive long enough to meet his Final Moment as ash rather than someone's midnight snack."

I flash him a puzzled look. I've never heard of the Ritus Cruciatus, never came across it in flipping through the tomes of ancient nonsense kept by Zeke, nor heard him speak of it. Granted, the list of ritus rumored to be included in the Corpus Rituum Perpetuorem—the fabled collection of rites belonging to the Everlasting and predating our division into Keepers and Praedari—is long, many of them outdated and more of them untranslatable. Whether it even exists as a literal item is debated, and whether it includes the variations of both sects is debated *bloodily*. Still, if such a sacred thing exists, it doesn't seem outrageous to think that Evelyn and the Council of Keepers might be in possession of it.

"The Ritus Cruciatus—basically a trial by rite," Caius explains. "A lot less *trial* than *rite*, though, and barbaric—even by the Praedari's standards. I'm not entirely surprised you've haven't heard of it. That's part of why I've come; the Council summoned me to assist in the Ritus. Few have seen the trial through to completion, and even fewer have the stomach for it. You've heard of the Salem Witch Trials, yes?"

"Sure." I nod.

"The role of the Inquisitor is to interrogate the accused, to torture from the accused a confession of wrongdoing—which then gives the Inquisitor the right to their Heartsblood," he explains, making air quotations around the word *right*.

"And if they're innocent?"

Though I ask, the answer matters little as far as

outcome. Victor can't claim innocence; he birthed Project Harvest into the world. With his confession, though, he could offer explanation. Not enough to free him from punishment, but maybe such that he could face a different fate. Does he know what awaits him? Is it too late?

A part of me resents the Council for what awaits Victor, as though they've sentenced him this way to rob me of having a choice in the way the rest of my unlife plays out. After all, why should I not take Zeke's seat on the Council if Victor has met his Final Moment? An archaic thought, but not so archaic to a Council of Elders. I am little more to them than Ezekiel's Childe—but to Victor? What *am* I to Victor?

He shakes his head, a barking laugh like a cough escaping his lips. "That's the thing, Delilah—there is no end to the Ritus Cruciatus that isn't the Final Moment of the accused. The interrogation doesn't determine whether one is guilty or innocent; the interrogation determines whether the Inquisitor bears the burden of consuming the Heartsblood of the accused." He pauses. "The Council's offer—you have a choice in all this, you know. Whether you would take his seat and what you would do with that power if you did."

[Evelyn's notes for Ritus Cruciatus, as transcribed by Nikolai Lockheart.]

THE COUNCIL OF KEEPERS HAS VOTED THAT I should start preparing the Ritus Cruciatus, and it is with heavy heart that I do so, Nikolai. This rite hasn't been voted into use in centuries and requires a unanimous vote of the Council of Keepers which is, as you can imagine, like herding cats.

And yet, here we are. [Sigh.] I know what you're thinking: if it requires a unanimous vote and I am so against it, why vote *for* it as surely I must have? Rarely are things that simple, Nikolai. If the

Praedari have what we think they have, the time has come for us to dust this one off and consolidate our power by undermining theirs. This rite is the difference between a scalpel and a nuke. Some in our sect would call it "restoring the balance" but don't let their niceties fool you; though it wears the guise of a sacred rite, it is nothing less than ceremonial genocide.

Perhaps to say *what we think they have* is incorrect, for it assumes a certain chronology and visions, divination, magics—they cannot be bound by time the same way you and I are. They are at once everywhere and nowhere, something and nothing, now and what was and what will be; like Schrodinger's Cat, paradoxical. So, *what we think they have* is *what we fear they might find* and *what they once had*—all at the same time. How do you prepare for every eventuality simultaneously?

When the time comes, I shall need the assistance of that brute, the Conqueror. Caius may be the only one among us who has administered the rites from start to finish. It takes a certain, shall we say, *strength of gut* to hear their confessions—and a certain distance from one's mortality to provoke them. To swallow down one's predator within will not suffice; one must bargain with it. The promise of Heartsblood is potent bait, but once the Beast is lured, then what?

The Addiction has claimed many an Inquisitor, and any who fall to it are not long for this world. How the Conqueror has managed to escape its hold I do not know. But I digress.

I daresay that even Enoch—ancient Enoch, Enoch who summoned Ismae the Bloody so she could be offered the position of Warlord—I daresay that even *he* has not himself administered the Ritus Cruciatus, though I would not be surprised to hear he had called for it more than once. You did not know that about Enoch, perhaps? He's lived far longer than any of us could ever hope to and it is my sincere belief that the day Enoch the Gray falls will mark the end of the Keepers.

Why? You're so predictable, Nikolai. I can hear your questions as you listen to this recording. Maybe I'm a *witch*?! [Laughter.] I will bore you with my theories about how long our kind can sustain two radically opposed ideologies another time, Nikolai. Spoiler alert (as you say): not forever.

Now, the Ritus Cruciatus seems to have two parts. This first part pertains to the Inquisitors, who must fast for a time sufficient to starve the predator within them. The idea is that by starving oneself, the Beast within us lurks just at the edge of consciousness, ready to devour anything with a heartbeat that dare show weakness.

[Pause.]

Well, I can see already why this isn't a popular rite. It says here the Inquisitors work in pairs so that the accused is given a *fair* trial—and I'll get to what *fair* means in this context later—but can you imagine two starving lions circling the same bloody steak?

Oh, strike *lions*—isn't that one of the Praedari's

slogans, "It's not the burden of the lion to protect the gazelle" or something? At any rate, perhaps it's not too crude an image, all things considered. I'm sure they have their own version of this rite, the brutality—yes, I've skimmed ahead—seems right in keeping with the spirit of their teachings.

So, the Inquisitors starve themselves and pair off. The Ritus Cruciatus is administered two-on-one—for the safety of the accused and the integrity of the rite—with the accused bound, but uninjured and fully sated.

Well, sure: I mean, if the rite relies on the cruelty of the Inquisitors, which in turn relies on them becoming one with their Beast-self, the accused should be: 1) showing weakness so as to provoke the violence we become capable of in this state, and 2) be healthy enough to endure the Inquisitors' wrath.

Texts suggest that sometimes the accused is tortured for several months in hopes of finally breaking them and hearing their confession. Of course, this could only happen if one of the Inquisitors finds themselves able to survive in this state without giving over to their predator within entirely.

According to my sources, this extreme example of the Ritus Cruciatus has been documented only once—can you guess the name of the Inquisitor attached to it, Nikolai?

Now

LYDIA ROLLS ONTO HER SIDE, VAGUELY AWARE OF the soft underneath her before the pounding in her head sets in, loud buzz from one ear tearing through the other. She whimpers. She smells her own blood which has soaked her shirt and jacket.

She tries to sit up but the buzzing slices through her head again and she grabs at her hair, burying her face in the pillow.

"What is it, my wildfire?" a familiar honeyed voice purrs from behind her at her bedside. "Wait, don't move. I'll come to you."

The scraping of a chair across the floor before

Temperance sits in her line of sight. Lydia hasn't seen her in a long time, yet the first thing she notices is her dress, the veil now tucked up underneath the knot of her updo, no longer obscuring her face as it had in Council chambers.

"Who died?" she groans.

"Almost certainly you, my wildfire," Temperance sighs, unpinning the veil from her hair and setting it on the nightstand. She leans in to brush a lock of hair from Lydia's bloody forehead. "He certainly did a number on you, didn't he?"

"Who?"

"Pierce, of course."

Lydia rolls onto her back, drawing the fluffy comforter to her chin. She's grateful the lights of the modest hotel room glow dim—small blessing, and almost certainly Temperance's doing. She was many things, but rarely inconsiderate.

"You're in a guest room at the hotel where the Council of Keepers has been headquartered for about a century, give or take a few decades,"

Temperance explains, anticipating her question. "I had Pierce retrieve you from the prison below—far below—where you awaited your fate."

"My fate?"

"A kind way of saying *punishment*," she offers. She dabs a washcloth in the glass of water on the nightstand and leans in to wipe away some of the blood on Lydia's face.

"Why are you telling me this?" Lydia challenges, narrowing her eyes. She jerks her head to avoid Temperance's touch but winces immediately with the sudden movement.

"What have I to lose by telling you the truth now?"

Lydia scoffs. "That's exactly what I told Kiley before I told her about Project Harvest. Now look at me."

Temperance merely smiles at this, wiping blood from Lydia's face. "There. That's better. Far more dignified."

"Well, what is my fate, then?" Lydia demands.

"The Ritus Cruciatus, a trial by rite. As I said, almost certainly death. Few who are innocent survive—and we both know you're not innocent." She frowns.

"Innocent of what?"

"You're accused of turning against the Keepers and helping the Praedari. Of treason, essentially. You attempted to aid in the resurrection of Ismae the Bloody—"

"The *resurrection*? Is that what the Keepers call it?"

"Well it is, isn't it? How long can one Slumber before losing themselves entirely? Anyway, you attempted to aid in the resurrection of Ismae the Bloody by kidnapping her mortal descendants for what you believed to be the rite that would awaken her. Am I missing anything?"

"Are you asking for my kill count?"

"Surely you wouldn't know something so vulgar, would you?"

Lydia taps her head. "It's not like I could forget."

"Ah, yes. My little eidetiker, the favored of my—" she trails off. "Even now," she adds with a sigh. Then she frowns: "I'm sorry you're burdened with such knowledge, my Childe. You will be free of it soon enough. Would you like something different to wear to your trial?"

Lydia shakes her head, the pounding having subsided. She pulls herself to sit up.

"Is Pierce yours, too?" she asks, more accusation than question though in truth she's not sure which answer she'd prefer.

Temperance can't help but laugh in reply. "Goodness, no! He's merely hired help—" She notices the brightening of Lydia's features and frowns again. "Haven't you figured it out, my Childe? Were you so starved for their love that you didn't put it together?"

Lydia feels the pressure in her chest of a breath held too long as she waits for her Usher to speak. Some bad news you know before you hear it, and at the same time could never summon the courage to speak aloud yourself.

"I told him to find you after you left me. I marked you with my Blood and let him do the rest."

"Was he supposed to kill me? Why not just kill me yourself like you were supposed to?"

Temperance shakes her head.

"Why?" Lydia demands, struggling to keep her voice level. "Why go to all that effort?"

"To protect you."

"*Why*? That doesn't answer why. The Council could have killed you."

"It wasn't an act of bravery. I knew they wouldn't subject me to the Ritus Cruciatus for betraying our sect because I sent Pierce to infiltrate. As far as the old Council saw, I set up an intricate tactical surveillance, the likes of which the Praedari would never think to unravel. Pull at one loose thread . . ."

She stands and crosses to the window, moving the curtains aside to look down on the city below.

"They thought me brilliant! Cold, but brilliant: to put my own Childe into play like any other pawn. I ate up their adoration, their praise, their accolades. They saw it as me vying for more of a voice on their Council, and when they offered it to me I did not decline."

She steals a glance behind her to Lydia, who sits up in the borrowed bed listening. She's drawn her knees up and rests her chin on them, arms hugging her bent legs. She's focused her Blood to heal the superficial head wound, her pallor still pale, of course, but only as much as on a good day.

"They named me their—oh, what does it matter? That's the thing about titles, we often forget their fluidity. Enoch Slumbered at the time, and everyone else fell to ash and was replaced. You were gone and Pierce with you. No one to remember. They knew you were my Childe, of course—etiquette deemed I remain open about that fact—though Enoch never drew attention to it. I suppose he couldn't, what with his history with Ismae."

She turns to Lydia.

"You know, old hotels like this used to have fire escapes. Not all were taken down to satisfy updated fire codes; some windows were merely replaced by hotel industry-standard ones, ones that are difficult—but not impossible—to shatter. A mortal with a fire extinguisher could manage it, sustaining some significant injury. I would imagine one of the Everlasting who inherited a bit more strength than others of the Blood could manage it themselves," she suggests with a shrug. "It would trigger the fire alarms, though, unless they were disabled for some reason. I think actually ours were malfunctioning earlier; I think despite Brantley's attempts to call in favors, the fire department was tending to something major on the other side of town—something about a Praedari riot," she pauses a beat. "We are at war, of course. You should rest before your trial.

The Keepers have provided me escort to return to Council chambers, as well as guards for your room."

She strides to the door of the room, the only sound her skirts rustling. She pauses with a hand on the doorknob, her skin mostly hidden by a black lace glove.

"Temperance?"

"Never have you feared death, Childe," she starts in a whisper. "Would that I could say the same."

21

Now

CAIUS TAKES HIS LEAVE AFTER SOME TIME. I PULL THE furniture roughly to where it was before I left, roll up the tarp, and shove it in a too-small kitchen trash can. I put water in the kettle and the kettle on the stove, drop a tea bag into a white ceramic mug stolen from a diner down the block. Zeke didn't have dishes when he Ushered me, had no need, but he stole the mug for me shortly after my Becoming and other things—the kettle, the trash can, a few towels—followed in short order. There wasn't much I retained of my former self, but something about the ritual of brewing a cup of tea, something about the wet-hot of steam on my face as I hover above its surface, kept me grounded, even in those tumultuous first nights. Even without memory to tether me, this ritual could pull me back from elsewhere.

I retrieve from the pile of stuff I left by the door when I arrived the oversized shoebox Victor gave me at Project Harvest, setting it on the coffee table in front of the couch next to another similarly sized box made of wood. Some of Zeke's things, the least hidden of his hidden artifacts. I run my hand over the lid of the box, the smooth grain of the wood.

The whistle of the kettle startles me. I pour the scalding water over the tea bag, take the mug in my hands, wait for the hot of the water to warm the ceramic, then my skin. This, the water boiling, sliding furniture around—everything feels in slow motion now, away from the chaos of the siege. Funny how so few moments can shape our perception.

Sitting on the couch I stare at the two boxes as though they might leap from the table and bite me.

I sigh. As I inhale the citrusy-floral scent of earl grey, I watch the tea in the mug ripple. Moments like this remind me of him: this apartment, the steam, the chair now bare of the drop cloth that had protected it from the splattering of my blood.

I sigh and sink to the floor, mug in hand, a large gulp of hot tea spilling over onto my skin with a sharp sear of pain. I set the mug down on the coffee table, leaving a ring of tea where it splashed over the lip of the mug. I pull the box Victor gave me towards me, feeling braver than I had either time I dug through its contents at Project Harvest.

Photos, notes, trinkets. I wonder how he has all this, why the things he wrote to me would be in this box, too, the second half of a conversation I've long since forgotten. I gather a stack of photos, cards, notes, laying to the side those things I've already combed through. My fingers grope inside, snatch up a small, dark pink collar with a partially rubbed-off black design, too worn to make out clearly what it was.

"Waffles," I say to no one, a smile playing at my lips. I lay the collar on the table next to my mug.

Next my fingers find the corner of a square of paper, a note folded thick. *Delilah! <3* in purple marker. I unfold the just-yellowing paper carefully, the same handwriting in the same color purple inside: *As you have known for quite awhile, I am now friends with Chloe, and well . . . She said I can't be your friend and hers. And don't hate me, but I chose her. We have been friends for awhile now and I . . . I'm ready to move on, you know? I know you'll miss me but this is goodbye . . . -Miya*

Miya? I purse my lips in concentration, again narrowing my eyes, as if my gaze could bore a hole through the note and into a memory long lost. How old was I? How did he come to have this? What was it Victor had said? *No one there liked you much.* Seems I started earning this reputation at a young age. I laugh softly to myself, folding up the note. Probably for the best I don't remember her, she seems like a little brat.

In the box I find some folded foreign bills, a few coins—currency from places I had traveled, perhaps, or wished to. Four of the folded-paper "fortune tellers," each scribbled on in different colors and in different handwriting; Victor's name appearing on each in what I've come to recognize as my younger self's handwriting.

I pull from the box a notebook with a hard, bright pink vinyl cover, *Journal* emblazoned across the front in glittery rainbow letters. An inscription in ballpoint pen inside the cover, dated April 5: *To my daughter, on her birthday. I've told them to let you sleep, for when you wake, you shall move mountains. (And because you're very crabby in the morning.) (Kidding!) Love, mom.* Tears well in my eyes, the weight of knowing I've outlived a mother who loved me dearly, but whom I can't remember, hitting me hard.

My fingers again find the thing I couldn't bear to open the last time I rifled through this collection of artifacts of my past: a small, hinged red velvet box. I turn it over in my hands before taking a deep breath and opening it. My jaw drops and I can't help but giggle into the empty apartment. Tucked in between two mounds of black velvet, a silver-colored ring with a single, tiny glint embedded in a star. I take the ring out and examine it before closing my hand around it protectively. In my other hand I take up Waffles' collar.

The ring had a note attached to its memory, a long time ago, which I fish from the box: *Dear Delilah, It has been a while now and . . . well can you just meet me at the fountin on your birthday in a few weeks? Thanks, Victor.* He had taped to it a wallet-sized photo of himself against the subtle blue gradient that each of us had as a backdrop for our school portrait that year. I had written a note back, the pink highlighter I used on the other side of the paper shadowing behind what he had written, faded now: *Oh Victor! It's great to hear from you, I would love to meet you there! Delilah.*

He kept it all these years: the ring he "proposed" to me with in fifth grade.

I reach for the second box, Zeke's box, which until now was resting undisturbed on the coffee table. If Victor's box contained my past, what would I find within this one?

ᔐᔑ

October 31, 1733

My dearest Ezekiel,

It is with heavy heart that I must ask a favor of you—the magnitude of which I will attempt to convey, but know that no words seem adequate. At best, your conduct will place you under scrutiny; at worst, you will be charged for treason by the Council of Keepers. I wish it could unfold any other way, but at present I am at a loss for other possible endings.

Tonight the veil between the mortal world and the world of the dead thins. Those of us walking without life exist alone in this in-between, unable to fully enter either world. Tonight the secrets of both the living and the dead spill into one another, intersecting in the in-between to form a crossroads forcing Seers to make a choice. This night I've had a vision, something I know you put little stock in, though I would be lying if I did not admit that I hope you grow to embrace that which we cannot know. Your unlife will be made that much richer for it. Try and open yourself to the unseen, the unknowable. Whether you choose to or not, it will find you. You will be drawn to it, like moth to flame—this I have seen. But I digress.

I must enter the Slumber.

The Crusader will come looking for me. He believes that by awakening me the Praedari will ascend to power, that I will rise up and join their cause—that I will again turn on the Keepers. He thinks he knows well my story and he does—the parts of my story still whispered among the Everlasting in those lightening hours before the sun overtakes the moon, at least. Like them, he knows well the carnage I've left in my wake but misunderstands what battle I fought and why. The Praedari look to me as a symbol of revolution; by awakening me The Crusader also believes he will earn their trust, that they will finally rally behind him in ushering in his vision.

But I never asked to be a part of their war.

When the time comes, I need you to lead The Crusader to me. I cannot tell you who he is for he has not yet been Ushered—indeed, he has not yet been born—but he will make himself known to you. Ezekiel, you must understand the gravity of what I ask of you. The Council of Keepers will see this as an act of treason. Even Enoch, the Eldest among them, may not yet understand why I turned on the sect instead of accepting the position of warlord those many years ago. There will be no amnesty for you in the bosom of the Council.

The Crusader must awaken me. I must restore the balance. While I feel no remorse for my actions at the founding of the two Sects—for regret, like most emotions, is a waste—tonight I make the choice to enter into contrition.

I know you will not let me down, Ezekiel. You will face a choice that night, as I have this All Hallows' Eve. Should our paths never again cross, know that your beloved, whom you've yet to meet, will find her way in your memory.

Eternally yours,

Ismae

22

Now

*H*E KNEW ALL ALONG.

I stand, flipping the coffee table in a mess of letters and photos and cold tea. The predator within me snarls and I stoop to pick up the now-empty mug, flinging it against a wall. It bursts into white ceramic shrapnel but I do not stop. I lunge for the couch, lifting it and tossing it against the outer wall of the apartment, dangerously close to the window but I do not notice. In one deft spin I knock down a floor lamp and the coat rack, sending the latter through the screen of the television.

Feathery entrails of pillows bathe the floor, couch, chair in fluffy carnage.

He knew all along and never told me.

A mess, but I am not yet satisfied—nor is she, the Beast within me that's stirred now and craves something warm and writhing to sink her fangs into. I storm into the bedroom and hastily throw things into a vintage suitcase: clothes, shoes, books, weapons. The dagger Zeke pulled off Tomas in the raid. Brittany's hairpin. I pass through the living room on my way to the front door, stopping on a whim to scoop up the contents of both boxes, now strewn, and shove them into the suitcase.

I didn't see it. I ruined everything—this whole thing could've been over if I'd just never gotten involved. Or if I'd done like the kid asked . . .

Hunter. Hunter understood what she failed to see. Hunter, who died to protect her so she could awaken Ismae. Ismae, now missing.

I have to find her. I have to fix this. It's the only way.

I hit every one of Zeke's hiding places, in the order of how asleep he probably thought I was when he turned to them in the hours near dawn: underneath floorboards, secured to the bottom of our ritual chest both inside and out, behind false backs of cabinets and closets, taped inside the tank of the toilet. I tear into the stashes of journals, notebooks, letters, and leather-bound books in dead languages; add to my suitcase these and some jewelry, a couple weapons, a deck of tarot cards. Things I don't know the significance of, except that he took the time to hide them—if not from me, then from someone else.

I slam the door behind me as I step into the hallway, hearing the fluttering of paper before I look to the source of the sound. A note taped to the door which I snatch, the top left corner tearing, still stuck to the dark wood grain with a bit of clear tape.

Hail fellow, well met. Dumpster behind Donut Emporium. Thursday, 5 A.M.

23

Now

KILEY CIRCLES THE BLOCK A FEW TIMES, ALL THE windows in her neighbors' houses either smashed in or out or boarded up, and not so much as the glow of a TV screen illuminating one of them from within. She pulls into her driveway, the wash of the headlights harsh against the white doors of the detached garage, so she turns them off. From here she can see that her family boarded up the windows on this side of the house, including her own on the second floor. She regrets declining Morgeaux's offer of company in favor of striking out on her own for her homecoming.

Silence would be an understatement, the sound of the car idling in the driveway enough to rattle her nerves so she shifts to park and cuts the engine. A bright red "2" painted across the front door. "6" a few houses down. "4" next door. Purple paint on one door marks "2"; three others are tagged similarly in blue. Survivor counts, she guesses, communicating to authorities how many living await rescue inside. Every zombie movie she's ever seen surges to memory, except what gutted this wasteland of a subdivision subsists on blood, not brains.

She climbs out of the car, leaves the door open. Maybe she should've come during the day but really it seemed like six of one, half a dozen of another: stay on the enemy's schedule, awake at night, so you're not caught unaware, or try to hide really well so you can sleep at night and move during the day when they're asleep. Of course, the third option is to never sleep—Morgeaux told them about entire cults offering respite from the war in the guise of so-called "meditative sleeplessness" or, as Morgeaux put it, solace in insanity.

She pauses at the door, hand on the knob. What if it's locked? They'd fled Project Harvest without warning, so she didn't have her house key. She could pry the boards off one of the windows—of course she knows exactly which one doesn't latch quite right, the one she snuck out of to get herself abducted in the first place—but prying it up with the crowbar in the trunk of the car she borrowed would be loud, might attract attention. She could ring the doorbell but without knowing who's inside she wouldn't want to risk it. Mom and Dad could be "2", but it could also be a couple of squatters armed to the teeth with a "shoot first, look second" mentality. And she couldn't blame them.

She takes a deep breath, turning the knob. Unlocked.

That should've been her first clue.

Without moonlight, Kiley has to rely on the pen-sized flashlight she's brought, snatched from the first aid kit in the trunk of her car. As soon as she presses the door shut, hears the comforting click of the latch, she presses the shaft of the light firmly between her fingers until the tip glows.

As she turns and scans the room with the dim light, her shoe crunches on broken glass. The round window on the door had been shattered before it was boarded up but her gaze doesn't linger there. Instead: on the overturned bookcase with its books strewn about, some covers torn, some bent, some splayed open a quarter through, halfway through, near the end; picture frames and vases and trophies in varied states of knocked over, fallen, shattered; a fractured mirror, the glass spiderwebbed, some pieces missing; the corner of the rug folded back on itself.

That should've been her second clue.

The arc of glow provided by the penlight only radiates a few feet but she worries that in contrast with the utter dark of the rest of the house it might be detected through cracks in the boarded-up windows so she clicks it off, waits several moments to let her eyes adjust to the darkness.

Normally she could've made it from the front door to the landing, up the stairs, and to her room backwards with a blindfold on. Now, though, she stumbles on the unfamiliar and misplaced domestic shrapnel and grunts, hears the *tink-tink* of shatter beneath her foot, the muffled grind of broken glass into the carpet. She shrugs to no one in the darkness—after all, what's one more broken picture frame?

She stumbles again, this time throwing an arm out to steady herself on the dark shape of the sofa but not quickly enough. Her chin smashes into the floor, driving her teeth into the flesh of her lip. She tastes blood. She pushes herself up to sitting, one palm pushing up from carpet, the other from— what's that? Leather? Laces? A boot?

That should've been her third clue.

Her breath catches in her throat.

That should've been her fourth clue.

Sometimes the body knows before the heart has a chance to catch up. Click-click and a faint circle of light emanates from the thing in her hand, a sticky film—of something?—between her skin and the hard plastic.

That should've been her fifth clue.

Her eyes start at the dark pool that's congealed on the carpet, flicker over boot and flesh and tweed—none of the colors make sense in the dim glow of the penlight—and don't stop to rest until they find the faint bluish-white of pearl around a throat against too much reddish-black.

She steadies herself, the hand not pinching on the penlight landing in more of the reddish-black sludge, cool and sticky and thick to the touch. The sharp inhale before the scream, an odor filling her nostrils—*that* should've been her first clue—and before the sound leaves her throat, hot-wet splashes from inside her onto the carpet. Again and again she heaves, her stomach muscles clenching.

Time passes, marked only by the occasional

splash of hot bile erupting from her lips onto the saturated carpet and her sobs. It's still dark out when she grabs the pearls around her mother's slashed-open throat with a yank and darts outside. The car door as she left it, yawning open, waiting for her.

The red "2" painted on her front door wasn't a survivor count: it was a kill count.

24

Now

IT IS TEMPERANCE WHO ESCORTS ME TO THE PRISON located so many floors beneath the lobby of the hotel. The elevator brings us as far as Sub-basement Three. From there, she leads us around the small loop that is this floor: twice around and on the third pass she stops abruptly in front of a section of wall that on our last two laps housed a dumbwaiter. She presses her hand to a brick and a doorway-sized section of wall swings inward. She continues our descent down many damp stone stairs, flashlight in hand.

Reminiscent more in structure and ambiance to

catacombs than a prison—perhaps this place *was* catacombs, remodeled by the Keepers to serve as a dungeon: earthen floor, earthen ceiling. Recesses in earthen walls, each not much larger than a closet, serve as cells, partitioned from the main chamber by thick steel bars. All empty, save for one.

"He was brought here to meet with you, at your request. I convinced the Council that arranging this meeting was the least we could offer for so abruptly *pulling you* from Project Harvest," Temperance explains in hushed tones, the underscored meaning of her words not lost.

I bite back the surge of anger that wells up in my chest and threatens to spill over. A shudder courses through me, not mine but that of my predator within as she drinks up my rage like blood from a mortal vessel. *Pulling* me from Project Harvest, of course, a generous reframing of what actually took place when the siege began. Were it not for the intel Pierce likely provided them when I arrived, they had no way of knowing that I was not captured, bound like Victor and the others are now to a tiny cell a mile below ground in some dungeon-bunker.

And had I not jammed into the flesh of my chest the brooch that Temperance gifted me? Had it not turned up at precisely the right moment in the lining of my purse? What if it had gotten lost or stolen, or slipped from my bag? Or if it had not been returned to me as an act of good faith by Victor?

Of course, a lot of this guesswork could've been avoided altogether had the Council told me there was another informant infiltrating the blood farm.

"After, he will remain and await the Ritus Cruciatus," Temperance whispers, answering a question I do not ask. "Other captured Praedari wait farther below ground."

She nudges me forward and into the large opening of the main chamber before taking leave and granting us privacy, retiring to the sub-basement to wait. I take a few steps, shuffle towards the only cell whose bars close over it entirely. In the dim light

I make out a shape leaning against a wall, head in hands, knees drawn to chest: Victor.

He lifts his head as I approach.

"Delilah?"

He scrambles to the bars as I lunge, snarling, for them. My face crashes against them with a hollow clang, a stream of blood running from my probably broken nose. I thrust my arms inside, grabbing for Victor, fingers grazing his soiled shirt. My knuckles whiten as I pull futilely on the bars horizontally, hoping to bend them that I might give myself enough space to reach him but he stumbles backwards out of arms' reach.

My fangs slide down as frustration gives way to desperation. I throw my weight downward, hoping to wrench the bars from the earthen ceiling but they do not give. I yank upwards, hoping they might pull from the earthen floor, but they do not yield.

"You!" I snarl again, slinking a few steps away in defeat. "You knew all along."

When he doesn't answer, I slam by body against

the bars: "You sent me there to die!" My voice echoes in the chamber.

"I swear I didn't." He puts his hands in front of him as if for protection, as if I might manage to break down the steel and space that separates us. "Delilah, I would never . . ."

"But you *did*!" I scream, tears stinging my eyes. "You sent me to that cellar . . . my heart and lung . . . for Ismae," I sob.

My sobs turn to growls as my Beast-self paces. I swear I can feel her shake her head and grin, as disappointed at the show of emotion as she is excited by how I teeter at the edge of losing control entirely.

"Delilah, *no*—"

But I cut him off. "Did you know Ezekiel Winter was my Usher?"

He nods.

"And did you know Ismae was *his*?"

He nods again.

"Then don't you *dare* tell me you didn't know I was her Blood," I hiss from clenched jaw.

"I did!" he admits, stepping again to the bars and wrapping his hands around them, his face near enough mine that I could lunge and tear it from his skull before he could react. "I knew that—but I didn't know the translation of the ritual we had was wrong. I didn't know she couldn't be Awakened by her mortal kin, Delilah. I didn't know we needed *you* for the rite." He bites his lip. "How *could* I have?"

I shake my head. "Don't. Don't play with me."

"Delilah, how could I have known that you would find us? That you would come—that you would *stay*?"

"I-I don't know . . . " I shake my head again.

"Delilah," he starts to speak again and I just shake my head.

Every time my name crosses the threshold of his lips, my anger wanes, tears splashing to my feet, the floor. Not a trick of his Blood, but of my heart. He fishes in his jeans' pocket for something, holding it out to me. A princess-cut diamond sparkles from where it rests on a white-gold band.

"Do you know what this is?"

I nod. "An en—en—"

"Engagement ring," he finishes what I cannot. "You left this in my casket at my funeral."

"I kept the ring with the star, the one you gave me in fifth grade when we got married under the monkey bars," I whisper, furrowing my brow. "I wore it in place of that one, after you died. Until—"

"Until the night of your Becoming. You'd taken it off to work," he explains.

"How did you get it? How did you get any of my stuff? From whom? Did you come looking for me?" The questions erupt from me like lava from a volcano, more accusations than anything logical.

"I recovered it when I hired a private investigator to help find you. He'd gone to your work. I couldn't risk showing up again myself because I'd already been snooping around where you worked— well, no one was comfortable answering too many questions. Apparently the coworkers you were living with had boxed up your belongings for a family member to claim, but no one came, so your boss told the private investigator to take it with him," he explains. "Delilah, this has been in my pocket since you showed up at Project Harvest."

Tears wet his eyes. Something like a knot hard in my chest, the heaviness of an anticipation I've felt before but long since forgotten.

"You came to that place looking for something, Delilah," he says softly. "And I think you stayed because you found it."

"Then why send me to the cellar?" I demand.

"To tell you why those kids were there under our protection, to show you the ritual and how we planned to Awaken your Grand-Usher, Blood of your Blood. I planned to reunite you with Ismae—I know that Zeke was important to you, that in losing him you lost a part of yourself. I wanted to be the one that took away some of that hurt. Delilah," he says through tears. "I want to pick up where we left off—before my Becoming, before my funeral. Before I messed everything up."

I sob, placing my hands on top of his around the bars, my lips finding his between them. A spark starts between my shoulders, traces down my spine. I'm the one who breaks our salty kiss with a sob, shaking my head as if in doing so I could force all doubts back to the recesses of my still heart.

"But the ritual. You needed my heart and lung . . ."

He shakes his head. "I would never hurt you. I was going to convince you to Usher someone so that we could Awaken her *together*, with *their* heart and *their* lung."

He continues, his gray eyes pleading. "Delilah, we can leave this place. You know the way here, and out. My Elders will help us relocate somewhere safe—or you don't even have to become Praedari. We'll fake our deaths, we'll go off-the-grid, away from everyone. No one will find either of us this time."

I find myself nodding along with his suggestion as he slips the ring onto my left ring finger, a perfect fit even after all these years. Maybe if I took Zeke's seat on the Council, I could speak out against the Ritus Cruciatus, speak on Victor's behalf. Maybe. *Maybe* feels so thick, trapping my tongue as voice echoes thought.

"Maybe," I whisper, a tear rolling down my cheek.

I press my lips to his again. He pauses a beat before recovering from surprise to find the mutual rhythm of our kiss. Several moments pass between us, stars burning up as red giants before they harden and cool to white dwarfs. I've grieved for him once, how many more times must I?

The rustling of skirts in the stairwell startles us apart. Some endings we write and some are written for us.

"Temperance is coming," I whisper. "I have to go."

25

Now

KILEY SLINKS AROUND TWO BUILDINGS, EACH LONG since abandoned and boarded up. A shutter on the side of the church creaks in the wind, so long in disrepair from a lack of church funds that it hangs there in defiance of the toll time's taken on the old building. The church still sees visitors on Sundays, though numbers dwindle and, in the aftermath of the war between the Keepers and Praedari, it's remained locked and boarded—but untouched by the Everlasting.

The schoolhouse likewise remains untouched by the vampires—and, even before, by the congregation. Its paint cracked and peeling, steps sagging and warped from years of sun-rain-snow-rain-sun: haunted rumors keeping even trespassers from tampering.

She sits on the steps of the schoolhouse which give a little under her weight. After what she's been through, the fear of some ghost children seems laughable.

Kiley hears a rustle come up along the side of the schoolhouse, behind her. She takes her mother's string of blood-stained pearls from her pocket, holding them as if praying the rosary. She does not turn to face the source of the sound, instead speaking:

"They're dead," she says flatly.

"I'm sorry . . . " Lydia comes around the steps to sit next to Kiley. She puts her arm around the girl and pulls her head to rest on her shoulder.

"*Hail Mary.* And to strengthen him an angel from heaven appeared to him," Kiley intones.

"Well, I'm certainly no angel," Lydia deflects. "But I can listen."

"*Hail Mary.* He was in such agony and he prayed so fervently that his sweat became like drops of blood falling on the ground."

"I can see that parochial education certainly paid off," Lydia teases.

"*Hail Mary.* The spirit is willing, but the flesh is weak."

"Kiley, what are you saying?"

"I don't want to be weak anymore, Lydia." Teardrops pitter-patter onto Lydia's shirt like rain.

"Why did you come here?" Lydia asks.

"I thought you—if you were alive, if you got away—that you might come back here."

"Looking for you?"

Kiley nods against Lydia's shoulder. "Was I wrong?"

"No. That's why I came as soon as I could," Lydia confirms.

Kiley lifts her head, turning slightly to face her.

"Lydia, I don't want to be weak anymore."

Lydia studies her friend a moment before reaching out and wiping tears from her cheeks.

"Do you know what you're asking, Kiley?"

Kiley nods. Lydia lets her fangs slide down, doesn't hide them.

Lydia leans in, brushing the girl's hair from her neck. Kiley finds herself aware of the lack of warm breath on her skin, breaking out in goosebumps as the rush of her heartbeat drums in her ears. She takes a deep breath and closes her eyes. Lydia's lips graze her neck and Kiley tenses, her shoulders rising, instinct. She winces. Lydia places a hand on the girl's right shoulder, signaling her to relax.

"Sorry I—" Kiley whispers, her eyes widening at the sharp of her friend's fangs in her neck.

Lydia takes three measured drinks, gulping the hot liquid. She wraps her arms around Kiley who struggles against her. What's human in her rising up and fighting what she's asked for. Several more long sips and she feels Kiley go limp in her arms, feels the warmth start to fade from her skin, feels the slowing of her heartbeat, the fading of it. She holds her dying friend tightly to her, fangs still buried in vein.

She could let the girl die. Right here on these steps she could watch the life fade from Kiley's eyes, watch death settle into her emptying veins. With it, the girl's pain over losing her family would fade, too, become nothing.

To grant her friend's wish means letting her choose to relive this grief for the rest of her life. Like when she lost Aurelie, except this time she controls someone else's grief, not her own.

She lays Kiley at the threshold of the schoolhouse door, at the top of the steps where they sat.

"Whatcha got there, dinner?" someone calls from the sidewalk, guffawing at their own joke with a choking sound.

Lydia looks up, greeted by a pockmarked face boasting a familiar, crooked-toothed grin.

"Johnny!" She launches herself from the second-to-last step and into his outstretched arms.

"Whoa!" he laughs, hugging her.

"We—I thought you were dead!"

He sets her down, tousles her hair.

"Dead? Nah. Actually, I feel pretty good," he says, dodging her swatting hand. "That Quinn lady said we were in—what did she call it? Asgard? It was all shadowy," he explains with a shrug. "Can't remember it too well, actually. But man, am I *hungry* . . ."

He takes a few steps towards Kiley, who, as if on cue, jolts upright, gasping.

"Leave her alone, Johnny," Lydia warns, hopping onto a step and placing herself between the two. "I just made her."

"Made her, huh?" Johnny's eyes dart between the two girls several times. Lydia, her hand on her too-large hunting knife, ready. Then to a pale and panicked Kiley who's scrambled to her knees to throw up what was left in her stomach, the sound of wet splashing on grass off the side of the stairs.

He shrugs. "Well, welcome to the pack, kid."

Now

NIGHTTIME BEHIND THE DONUT EMPORIUM AND A seedy dive bar, the dumpsters. The smell of dough and wet pavement. I've been here too often in memory, in vision, this place perhaps the only thing left of him, of us, untouched by half-truths. Even in the aftermath of war, some things don't change. I know I'm waiting for shadow and shadow doesn't disappoint, dripping like oil from underneath the dumpster, pooling.

A raven forms from the pool of shadow and from the shadow-raven, a woman: her red hair in her usual messy braids, sword and shield, Dr. Martens.

Quinn, but she wears bloodied tatters, her skin covered in faint shadow-traces of Nordic tattoos— almost transparent, like watercolors. She wears a raven skull, a headdress of bone and feathers. The woman from the painting.

Tonight she seems illuminated from within, casting a glow onto the pavement that refracts in the sword and shield, sending a scatter like stardust at her feet. For a moment I think the pavement of the alley has become blood, but I blink and the pavement is just pavement.

"Hail fellow, well met," she smiles.

"You look different," I remark.

"And yet the same, yes? I've allowed some of Asgard to follow me into your world tonight. You are seeing the shadow of my Asgardian form, as much of it as I can bring into this place. Magic doesn't always travel well."

"What do you want?" I ask, crossing my arms over my chest.

"I've come to offer you a choice."

I snort. "Like you *offered* Zeke a choice? You've asked me here to kill me?"

"Ezekiel Winter made a choice, yes—but it is not the same I offer you."

She takes a deep breath, shadow-wriggling from places in the alley I hadn't noticed shadow, drawn to her. Shadow swallows her sword and her shield as she draws herself to her full height—no, taller, somehow, as if augmented by magic. The tattoos on her skin glow as the sword and shield she once held and no longer holds.

Her voice fills the night with the cadence of something like prayer: "Delilah, I've come to offer you a place in Asgard, that you may bear the Honored Dead to Valhalla. We've followed you for quite some time now, Oracle. It is time to come home—to take your place amongst the Valkyries, the Choosers of the Slain."

I do not answer, instead draw from my purse two objects which I hold out to her: two engraved silver arm rings, all that remains of the brother and sister with whom she shared a womb. She takes them from me, holding each close to her face in turn, her eyes tracing the runes as if they might tell the story of their Final Moments.

She clutches one in each hand, thrusting her arms out towards me. Then, she rotates her fists upward, opening her hands to show her palms. As she does so, the band in each hand erupts in flickering flame, hovering just a centimeter above her flesh. If it hurts, she does not wince.

"These mark the past, Delilah; the end of Liam and Mina's story. What I ask is what ending you will choose for your own?"

Her gaze falls to the ring on my finger. She balls her hands into fists again, this time extinguishing the flame. When she opens them, a black feather rests on each palm for a second before drifting to the black of the pavement beneath.

"I know the decision you must make, Oracle. Honor the memory of your Beloved and take his seat on the Council. Rescue one whom you've

loved, and who loves you, from his Final Moment."
A slight dip of her head indicates the ring as she
continues. "Or what I offer, where there is no love
save that between Sisters."

I slip the ring from my finger, tears stinging my
eyes. I step towards Quinn, my palm outstretched.
Her hand meets mine, deftly palming the ring as
she pulls me against her, chest to chest. She pats me
on the back twice with a solid *thunk-thunk*, a hug
between warriors. Tears sting pathways down my
cheeks.

"This doesn't change anything between us," I
whisper as the shadows of Asgard swallow us both.